TEN TALES OF TERROR

By
James Kennedy

Contents subject to copyright © 2013 James Kennedy

All rights reserved.

Cover photograph reproduced by kind permission of
Sean Johnson http://www.sxc.hu/profile/seanj

First Edition.

ISBN 978-1-291-32019-0

MOLESLY MANOR

CHAPTER ONE

  My name is Jacob Bambridge and I want to tell this story before I join my dear wife, who I lost three winters ago in the Big Freeze.
The ground was so hard that it took two men with picks and shovels half a day to dig her grave!
I am seventy three this Michaelmass and am becoming feeble; having to be helped by my neighbours to get in the wood for my fire and they are very kind in lots of ways. Anyhow that is not telling you the story; the year was eighteen hundred and twenty and the Prince Regent had come to the throne because Farmer George had lost his wits again, poor old man!
Napoleon had been beaten at Waterloo and was exiled to Saint Helena, leaving the world a sorry place full of widows grieving for their men folk.
Our village of Molesly at that time contained about one hundred and fifty souls; although our schoolmaster said that it was much bigger before the plague years.
 Many soldiers were straggling back home at that time and we had a couple settle in the village.
One was called Silence, an odd name, which he lived up to being very reserved in his manner; he became our blacksmith.
The other one, who's name was Grimes was a very odd fellow indeed!
Someone said that he had been blown up at Waterloo and it had affected his mind; it had certainly affected his left leg which was no longer there and he stumped about on a timber one!

However he did not let this disability stand in his way, he as always cheery and hard working in his trade which was as the village baker.
He would go about the village in a top hat which he claimed 'Nosey' had given him, that is the Duke of Wellington!
We always took what he said with a large pinch of salt as he was a great leg puller!

On a Friday evening we would play dominoes in the Snug at the Rose and Crown, a cosy old place with mullioned windows and a low beamed ceiling.
In the winter there was always a log fire burning in the great fireplace and we friends would sit round it drinking mulled ale and yarning the evening away until the landlord called time on us and we made our way home.

The Friday night before Christmas we got round to talking about ghosts and hauntings; why I don't know, it just seemed to happen as these things sometimes will, Perhaps it was because of the Season!
Anyhow, Mr.Cartwright the schoolmaster, who had been gazing into the fire and listening to our conversation suddenly said; "I'm surprised none of you have mentioned the hauntings at Molsely Manor!"
We turned to look at him in surprise as he did not often join in our circle being somewhat aloof; I expect being a learned man he found our chatter uninteresting; however this subject seemed to grip him and when pressed to tell us more about it he became quite animated.

CHAPTER TWO

"The Manor House, which was moated, was built in the early sixteenth century by the noble Delacourt family;" he said.
"They could trace their lineage to the Kings of France and were highly placed at Court!"
"Where is this Manor House?" I asked being unaware of any such place in our locality.
The schoolmaster smiled and said; "It never ceases to amaze me how village folk seem to know so little about their own history; why man you pass it every day on your way into the village!"
"You would probably know it better as Sir Humphrey's wood"
"What that dark old spinney opposite the church?" I cried; "the one that no poacher's dog will ever go into."
"The very same," replied Mr.Cartwright; " there are remains of the building; although the moat has dried up over the years and the whole thing is overgrown and neglected."
We were all astonished at these revelations, especially me as I had lived all my life in this place and never once had it been mentioned!

"What about these hauntings you spoke of," said Grimes, his top hat askew over his forehead and his timber leg thrust out dangerously near to the fire.
"Well it came about that at the death of Sir Humphrey's father, old Sir Henry, the Estates were divided up between four different branches of the family; part of Sir Humphrey's inheritance was the Manor house and the surrounding tracts of land, which in those days were largely for hunting; apart from the land around Molesly village and the common!"

"Sir Humphry was a bitter disappointment to his father, being a wild and rebellious youth; inclined to get into disputes with other landowners and had a roving eye for a pretty wench; which did not make him popular with the fathers of the local girls!"

"The consequence of this inheritance was that he grew even more wild and irresponsible; now he had a 'bolt hole' in the wood that he could withdraw to when things got too hot and no father to keep him in check. His hunting horn could be heard at any time of day or night and the superstitious would cross themselves and hurry home."

He surrounded himself with a rabble of dissolute young nobles and soon rumours of unholy goings on at the Manor started to go round the County; especially when two young girls disappeared from the village!"

"News of this outrage must have reached the ears of the King for the next thing was that Sir Humphrey and his cronies were sent abroad to fight in foreign wars and the Manor was left empty except for a retainer and his wife."

"They only stayed for a week then moved into the village because the wife said the place was haunted.

"She claimed that there were noises that could not be explained; like someone walking up the stairs and slamming doors, strange draughts rushing through the house and on occasion sudden icy coldness in a room even with the fire on!"

"Their dog ran off on the first day they arrived and never returned; also no bird sang in the wood!"

Cartwright stopped at this point, licked his lips and looked pointedly at his empty tankard which was immediately filled for him.

CHAPTER THREE.

After taking a long draught he continued; "Sir Humphrey came back after six years with a Blackamoor for company, having lost most of his companions in the wars.
He had also lost one eye and wore a patch which made him look more villainous that before!
He moved back into the Manor, but became a recluse and was seldom seen outside of the grounds.
The Moor on the other hand often came into the village and was a source of curiosity to us as we were not used to foreigners.
He spoke English better than most of us and seemed very learned, but there was something about him which unsettled folks; with his hooked nose and piercing dark eyes he seemed to look into your very soul and draw it out of you!
He would ask the local carrier to pick up and deliver items to the Manor; things which Boulter the carrier could not make out; being mainly chemicals and strange earthenware and glass vessels.
There was much speculation in the village as to what he and Sir Humphrey were up to, but no one could enlighten us.
Whatever it was seemed to involve complete secrecy and the outlay of a great deal of money!

One evening in his cups Boulter let slip that once when he was collecting a delivery for the Manor from London he had got into conversation with a warehouse clerk.
This man told him that they were the sort of things that were used by Alchemists; when Boulter asked what that meant the man laughed and said; "why someone who changes base metals into gold!"

There was great excitement in the village and speculation as to whether Sir Humphrey would succeed, but as some wiseacre remarked; "You don't think that he will share his bounty with us do you, the Gentry don't do that!"

However the speculation grew and reached a head one night when the local poacher, 'Darky' Mears said he was going over to the Manor to see for himself and challenged us all to accompany him!

He was a fearless fellow; well versed in the art of moving about at night and so far had never been caught, although everyone knew his trade.

Needless to say there were no takers and he said; "Very well I'll have to go on my own since none of you have the nerve!"

That was the last we ever saw of him; he never came back from that night's visit to the Manor!!

A search was organised and the local constable visited the place, but was told that Mears had not been seen and that if he had he would have been apprehended for trespass!

So the years went by and things settled down; past events faded from people's memories; although no one would willingly go past the wood at night.

CHAPTER FOUR

One evening in late November the whole village was awakened by a great explosion and flames could be seen in Sir Humphrey's wood.
Every able bodied man grabbed a bucket and ran towards the Manor.
The sight that met their eyes was awful; the West wing of the Manor House was well alight and a large part of the roof was missing!

A bucket chain was formed with water from the moat; several of the braver souls broke into the house.
They eventually found Sir Humphrey lying on the floor in the hallway; he was dead and had been badly mutilated by the fire; of the Moor there was no sign despite a thorough search after the fire was put out!
The seat of the fire had obviously been in a large room upstairs ; which although badly charred contained what was left of a smelting oven and various retorts and vats.
There were also several large books with strange symbols on the cover; one of which the Vicar said was a Grimoire and that it's cover was human skin!
The most frightening discovery was a large Wall painting of the devil surrounded by pictures of the sun and moon and other strange symbols set against a dark sky!
Sir Humphry was interred in the family vault in Essex; which we were very relieved about as we did not particularly want him in the local churchyard with his evil reputation!

Soon stories began to circulate about strange lights and noises coming from the Manor and people shunned the place even more!

One night a couple of youths who should have known better boasted that they weren't afraid of ghoulies or ghosties and were going to search for Sir Humphry's gold; after plenty of Dutch courage at the Rose and Crown they set off with spades and a sack to the Manor.

CHAPTER FIVE

 They had not returned by the next morning so with great foreboding a group of villagers set out to find them.
They were discovered in front of the wall painting in the upper room cowering on the floor babbling incoherently and their hair had turned white!
What they had seen or heard we never found out as they never recovered and spent the rest of their days in the local asylum for the insane.
From that day onwards no one ever thought of going into the wood as we were all afraid of the consequences!

 However some years later on a day in early Spring a smart yellow gig with two matching greys in harness rolled into Molesly and stopped at the Rose and Crown.
A powerfully built man stepped down from the gig and hailed the landlord; he was dressed in clothes of the latest fashion with silver buckled shoes and was wearing a periwig.
In fact if it hadn't been for his weather beaten face and broken nose he could have been taken for a dandy!
Sitting in the gig was a pretty, petite woman with long titian hair and an angelic face; she was holding a silk parasol and wore white gloves on her delicate little hands."
My name is Sir Peregrine Coombes and I would like directions to Molesly Manor;"he said to the landlord in a commanding voice.
The landlord was overawed by this authorative personality; he was not used to dealing with Gentry. Stumbling over his words he replied; "if it please your Honour the Manor lies opposite the church in Sir Humphrey's wood, but is not habitable sir!"

"I am well aware of that;" snapped Sir Perry, "I have acquired it and intend to rebuild it as our home; as he said it he looked over to his wife and smiled; turning back to the landlord he said; "have you rooms we could use whilst we look for suitable accommodation during the rebuilding?"

The landlord gulped and replied; "certainly sir; I will get my wife to prepare them at once; and when would your Lordship require a meal?"

We will return around six of the clock," responded Sir Perry; pray have something ready for seven!"

With that he climbed back into the gig, whipped up the horses and bowled off up the street towards the church!

CHAPTER SIX

Word soon spread around the village about this new development and there was much shaking of heads by the wiseacres who said it would all end in tears!
Sir Perry seemed to be a very determined man and when he found that none of the local tradesmen would venture near the place because of its evil reputation he hired men from Norwich to come out and work for him.
"You are a very independent lot in this place;" he said to George Bullen the local builder.
"That may be sir;" he replied, but all the money in the world would not draw me to work on that accursed place."
"I don't believe in such superstitious nonsense," said Sir Perry; "I have heard certain wild tales about the Manor and have put them down to idle speculation!"
"Well there are two men in the insane asylum who might not agree with you sir and several people missing who were connected with it!" responded Bullen finishing his drink and bidding Sir Perry good day!
Perry looked thoughtful for a while then shrugged and went up to his rooms.

Work on the restoration of the Manor went on apace and come the Autumn it was ready for occupation.
The furnishings had been installed and the staff were bustling about the place readying it for the Master and his lady to arrive.
The smell of cooking emanated from the kitchens and the dining room was a picture; with the long mahogany table laid out with crystal and silver and set pieces of flowers about the room.

The butler came down the hall shouting; "into your places ready to meet the Master and his lady; footmen to the main door to welcome them, the rest of you in the main hall!"

He strode back to stand on the steps to greet Sir Perry and his lady who were just arriving at the front portico where they alighted from the carriage.

The Butler came down the steps to greet them; "Welcome to Molesly Manor to you and your lady Sir Peregrine; I have taken the liberty of gathering the staff in the hall so that you may meet them, I know they are all looking forward to it sir!"

"In that case we mustn't disappoint them; lead on Manners said Perry with a wry smile offering his arm for his wife to rest on as they went into the house!

CHAPTER SEVEN

Sir Peregrine Coombs was a self made man; in that he had been left a substantial sum of money by an elderly aunt; he chose to put it to good use by buying up land in Jamaica and developing a thriving sugar plantation there.

He had by dint of hard work and the judicious purchase of further parcels of land increased his holdings to such a degree that he became one of the largest landowners in the West Indies and was much respected by the other plantation holders.

So much so that he was appointed Governor of that island and was renowned for his fairness and firmness in settling local disputes.

It was during this time that he met his future wife Shivaughn the daughter of an Irish émigré from Connnaught.

Patrick O'Malley was a large, bluff, hard drinking, jovial fellow with a booming voice who doted on his only child; having lost his wife due to a fever shortly after arriving in Kingston.

He ran the largest haulage firm in Jamaica and his wagons transported the processed sugar from the plantations to the docks.

Perry had met Shivaughn at her father's house during a call to discuss business; whilst awaiting O'Malley's arrival had cause to look into the room in which she was accompanying herself on the harpsichord and singing a particular old Irish ballad

He was captivated both by her beauty and her sweet voice and it was love at first sight!

He asked her father if he could escort her to the Planters Ball in Kingston and they soon became inseparable; often seen together driving through town in his carriage.

Realising that his love was returned he formally
proposed and was accepted much to his delight!
They were married in Kingston by the Bishop and the
whole of the island's society turned out to celebrate the
happy event.

   They settled down at Providence, his large house on
the plantation to an idyllic state of married bliss; riding
out each day in the green tropical countryside.
Shivaughn was enchanted by the tiny humming birds;
like living jewels darting amongst the flowers whilst
they drew the nectar with their long beaks!
She would clap her tiny hands in joy at the bright
colours of the troops of noisy Macaws in the trees
squabbling over the fruit they were feeding on!
He would draw her to him as they sat on the porch
watching the sun going down into the sea and as dusk
stole in like a thief to envelope the land.
He was filled with peace and contentment as he held
her close and the scent of her hair filled his nostrils;
what more could a man want of life, this was heaven on
earth!

CHAPTER EIGHT

   The following year a devastating hurricane hit the island and the sugar crop was badly affected, Shivaughn lost her baby and was ill for some time afterwards!
She slowly started to mend physically; but it was obvious that the loss of the child had caused her to be low in spirits.
The doctor drew Perry aside one morning and said; "If you will take my advice you will consider taking your wife away from here; preferably to a cooler climate."
"The temperatures and infections of the West Indies will not be safe or suitable for her if you wish to have more children!"
Perry was stunned and protested; "This is our home and my business and social responsibilities are in the island!"
"Well of course the final decision is yours;" responded the doctor; "but as a friend as well as your doctor I strongly advise you to think carefully where your main responsibility lies!"

   Perry rode out to the hilltop overlooking the plantation and looked over his land; noting the great swathes that the hurricane had cut through his crops; but the words of his doctor kept coming back again and again; he finally realised that he had no choice!
He put his Agent in overall charge of the plantation, with the requirement that he was to be advised once a month of the progress of the business while he was in England.
He also asked his father in law to keep a watching brief in case things went wrong.

O'Malley was devastated on hearing they were leaving the island. "Mother o God; I'm goin' to be left all on me own; the light of me life is leavin' me and off to England of all places!"

He was inconsolable and embarked on a three day drinking bout; after which Perry had to use all his persuasion to persuade him to accept the situation for his daughter's sake.

Eventually he was persuaded; but said "I shan't be comin' to see me grandchildren in that Godforsaken land; tis a bunch of heathen's ye are!"

With that he grabbed Perry in a bear like hug and said; "Look after her son; she's all I've got to remind me of her dear mother; God rest her."

With that he turned away so Perry wouldn't see his tears and made for the whiskey bottle

CHAPTER NINE

At first things at the Manor seemed to go well and the couple continued to be happy in each others company; but then Shivaughn started to have strange dreams bordering on nightmares.
In them she would often see, advancing down a long corridor, a tall sinister black man clad in a cloak covered in strange symbols picked out in silver wire; a black turban and red Moroccan slippers on his feet.
He had piercing black eyes, a hooked nose and a twisted smile; as he walked towards her he opened his arms as if to embrace her; but at this point she always woke up shaking with fear!
She told Perry one night about the dreams and he was most concerned in case her depression after the loss of the child was returning.
He called in the local doctor who gave her a thorough examination, but could find no immediate reason for her state of mind.
"I cannot detect any underlying cause Sir;" he said; "however I will prescribe something to help her to sleep and call again to observe her progress!"

Time passed and the dreams seemed to recede; but she told Perry that she felt as if she was being watched and that one or two personal objects had gone missing from her dressing table.
"It may seem trivial;" she said; "but in Jamaica if the Obeah woman wants to put a spell on someone they always take something personal to gain power over them!"
Perry tried to make light of it; laughing he took her in his arms and said; "you have a wonderful imagination my pet; but it just might be that you have a light fingered maid!"

Shivaughn would not hear a word against Blanche her personal maid whom she liked and trusted; "In fact it was she who drew my attention to the missing items;" she said.

"Well I don't think that we have anyone in the household who looks in the least like an Obeah; unless you count Mrs. Ward the housekeeper; she's a formidable lady;" chuckled Perry/

"You will not take seriously anything I say, will you;" she said, laughing in spite of herself.

CHAPTER TEN

Odd things happened over the next few weeks; one of the housemaids was working in the West wing preparing rooms for some of Perry's guests when she thought she saw a figure walk across the hall outside the room!
Thinking it was one of the guests returning she gathered up her cleaning utensils and went out into the corridor; there was no one there, but she swore that she heard footsteps coming past where she stood!
She was badly frightened and refused to go there on her own.

One night in November there was a terrible storm which seemed to roll around the Manor most of the night and the occupants were denied any sleep by the continuous lightning flashes and crashes of thunder.
One of the footmen had gone down to the kitchen to fetch himself a drink; as he walked in through the door holding a lantern the light reflected off a pair of eyes at the far end of the kitchen table.
He fled and his cries roused the whole household and Sir Perry came out of his bedroom carrying a lighted candle in one hand and a loaded pistol in the other!
After giving the terrified man a brandy he calmed the man down sufficiently to describe what had happened.
Quickly Perry and several of the male servants went to the kitchen to apprehend the intruder.
There was no sign of anyone or of anything missing; Perry ordered the servants to check the doors and windows downstairs for forced entry; but again without result.
Everyone went back to bed, but few of them slept!

Rumours started to circulate amongst the staff that the place was haunted and two of them gave notice! Perry decided that he must nip the rumour in the bud at once or more would follow; so he held a meeting at which he assured them that there were no such things as ghosts and that the house was old, which probably was the cause of strange noises; draughts in corridors etc!

He persuaded the two to cancel their notice and raised everyone's wages; this seemed to settle the matter and things returned to normal once more.

CHAPTER ELEVEN

Mr. Cartwright was cut short by the landlord calling time; "come along gentlemen have ye got no homes to go to?"
"I would be obliged if you would drink up and return to them," with that he purposefully shut the serving hatch and went to his living quarters!
The schoolmaster sighed and said; "well my friends you will have to wait for another evening for the rest of the story; Good night to ye!"
Grimes walked up the road with me till we reached the bakery; as we stopped the church clock chimed the midnight hour; "another two hours and I shall have to be up to light my oven;" mused Grimes.
I carried on up the road reflecting on the amazing tale that had unfolded this evening and could not wait for the continuation of it!
As I passed the church a white shape floated silently past me, it was a Barn Owl on its way to hunt in Sir Humphrey's wood.

It was not to be until after Christmas that we saw the schoolmaster again; apparently he had relatives in Aylsham and had spent a few days with them over the Festive Season!
Silence was not with us that night as he had strained himself shoeing one of farmer Inglestone's heavy horses; a common complaint amongst blacksmiths.
We were in good spirits as we had been sampling a barrel of old ale, which the landlord had acquired to celebrate the season.
Mr. Cartwright picked up the story from where he had left off; after his glass had been topped up of course!

Much to their delight Perry and Shivaughn found that she was pregnant again!

"You must take care and have plenty of rest; we don't want to lose this one," said Perry.

"You would have me wrapped in cotton wool if you could;" she laughed, "I want to live a normal life and enjoy it; let us have a Ball and invite everyone so they can share in our good fortune!"

Invitations were sent out far and wide to the local gentry and professional people that Perry had dealings with; also the local incumbent at the village church, with whom they had made friends, the Reverent Josiah Grimshaw, who was also an antiquarian and student of local history.

His wife was an outgoing lady who had studied music and played the violin and cello as well as the church organ for the services!

On the night of the Ball the Manor was ablaze with light and the drive was constantly busy with carriages arriving and people in all their finery alighting and climbing the steps to be announced by Manners the butler.

As the guests were ushered into the banqueting hall they were shown to their places at the great mahogany tables, covered in white damask tablecloths, the array of silverware and the monogrammed plates, tureens, sauce boats, crystal glasses and decanters were breathtaking!

Each place setting was named and were so arranged that everyone had a member of the opposite sex facing them!

The gong sounded and everyone took their place at the tables; unwrapping their serviettes ready for the first course which was Mulligatawny soup.

Whilst this was being served the wine waiters were bustling about the room ensuring everyone had the wine they required.
The buzz of conversation intermingled with the clink of glasses and the sound of spoons contacting plates filled the room and Perry and his wife looked on with pleasure at such a happy scene!

When the many courses of the banquet were finished and a suitable interval had elapsed every one withdrew into an adjacent room to allow the servants to clear everything away so that the dancing could commence.
There were five musicians seated on a dais at the end of the room, one of whom was Mrs Grimshaw on the violin.
They struck up a waltz and soon the floor was full of couples whirling around under the beautiful chandeliers; led by Perry and his glowing wife.
She was deliriously happy and made the most of every moment, finally sitting breathlessly down whilst Perry went to fetch them some punch.
Several female acquaintances came over to talk about the forthcoming baby and to congratulate her and wish her well.
Perry returned with the cups of punch and they chatted as they watched the dancing and sipped their drinks.
After a suitable interval they were on the dance floor again to form up for the 'Roger de Coverly' and the 'Gay Gordons'; the dancing went on until at midnight the Ball came to a happy end and Perry and his bride stood at the portico bidding their guests farewell.

The air was chill and suddenly Shivaughn shivered; she slipped her hand in Perry's
and said; "I'll be back in a moment I must have left my wrap in the ballroom!"

So saying she entered the empty room and walked across to the chair where sure enough there it lay. She had a feeling that she was being watched and looked up; at the end of the room was the old minstrel's gallery, standing half concealed in the shadows was the Moor!

CHAPTER TWELVE

Perry had said goodbye to everyone and suddenly wondered where his wife had got to; she had only gone to get her wrap and should have returned some time ago!
Concerned for her welfare he hurried back to the ballroom, but she was nowhere to be seen, thinking that she may have been taken ill he ran up the stairs to their rooms, but she was not there either!
He had a feeling of foreboding which he could not explain and rushed downstairs calling out for the butler who came from the pantry.
"You called sir?" Manners inquired.
"Yes; have you seen Lady Coombes recently?" Perry asked.
"Why no sir; I have been working in the pantry since the guests left; but I will enquire amongst the servants as sometimes her Ladyship goes into the kitchen to instruct cook about forthcoming menus sir.
Perry dashed down to the kitchen causing the staff to jump to their feet embarrassed by his sudden arrival!
"It's all right I've come down looking for my wife, have you seen her?"
They all shook their heads and replied that they had not!
Right, then I want you all to start searching the house as in her present condition she may have fallen or fainted somewhere and the sooner we find her the happier I shall be!
He took two footmen with him and went down to the cellars which ran under the length of the house; they all carried lanterns and searched every nook and cranny of the place without success.

The footmen had gone ahead up the stairs; but Perry was still searching behind the racks when he noticed something odd.
There were a set of footprints in the dust going towards the wall, but none returning!

CHAPTER THIRTEEN

He held the lantern up to the wall and noticed there was a groove in the stone where slabs met: putting his hand in the groove he felt a metal catch.
Pushing it caused a section of the wall to swing open exposing a large tunnel; he fancied that he could hear some kind of chanting coming from a long way off.
Without further ado he raised his lantern and walked inside; suddenly something fluttered past his face, then another and another; bats, scores of them!
He pushed on towards the sound of the chanting; also he could see light further down the tunnel.
Cautiously he reached the source of the light and looked into a room; the sight that met his eyes was unbelievable!

He was looking into a high arched room with a flagstone floor; which on one side had a series of tables covered with retorts, phials, large dark coloured jars with gold lettering on them, a smelting oven with a big clay condenser over it; weighing scales and everything that is required in Alchemy!
In the centre of the room stood the Moor, wearing only a cloak covered in Cabalistic signs.
He was standing in the centre of a Pentacle which had been outlined in white on the floor.
Around the outside of the Pentacle at intervals, black candles burned, whilst inside there was a lectern with a large book covered in what looked like leather!
The Moor stood at full height with his arms raised; in his right hand he held a metal wand and in the other a sword!
He continued chanting in a language that Perry recognised as Arabic and the name Baphomet was frequently mentioned.

"The man is trying to raise one of Satan's Demons;" muttered Perry, and as he spoke he noticed the room was darkening.

Then his heart missed a beat as he saw a thin tendril of black smoke beginning to curl up from between the flagstones and start to form a shape which was not human!

Perry was rooted to the spot; he had seen magic rituals performed by the slaves in Jamaica, but this was beyond his comprehension and he felt afraid; this was pure evil!

The smoke continued to build until it seemed to become solid finally forming into a gigantic goat which looked down on the Moor expectantly.

The room was now bitterly cold and the Moor abased himself before the creature, then came out of the Pentacle and walked over to a curtained alcove.

CHAPTER FOURTEEN

The Moor drew back the curtain exposing a large stone slab; on this was a woman clad in a white shift; suddenly Perry's blood ran cold and he almost fainted, the woman was his wife!
By now the Moor had reached the slab and picking up a curved dagger he turned to Shivaughn.
Raising the dagger above his head he began chanting again; Perry broke out of his trance; he had to save her, he rushed into the room and threw his lantern straight at the Demon.
As the lantern reached the figure there was a great explosion and a rush of foul air which
knocked Perry against the wall driving the breath out of him.
The lantern had passed through Baphomet and landed amongst the chemicals strewn on the benches; there was a blinding flash and a fire began to consume the room!
Recovering, Perry rushed to rescue Shivaughn and swept her into his arms; her skin was as cold as marble, but she was breathing; "Thank God," he said as he made for the tunnel.
Barring his way was the Moor, his face contorted with rage; "you will not escape me infidel," he hissed, "you have destroyed a life's work with your meddling; the Philosopher's Stone and the Elixir of Life were almost within my grasp and now I am condemned to the Abyss!"
As he was talking Perry noticed that a tongue of flame was creeping up the back of man's cloak!
Suddenly the Moor became aware that he was on fire; dropping the knife he started beating at the flames; but they had got a hold and he began rushing round the room screaming.

Perry was sickened, but there was nothing he could do; the fire by now was burning fiercely and his first priority was to get his wife out of danger.
As he ran down the tunnel the fire seemed to be following like a living thing, throwing out tendrils as if trying to catch him.

Fortunately the door was still open and he ran through the cellars and up to the ground floor.
One of the footmen saw him and helped him to lay Shivaughn on a chaise.
Perry got his breath back and shouted, "get everyone out into the grounds, there's a fire raging down there and it will soon engulf the house!"
As he spoke first smoke began billowing out of the cellar door followed by tongues of flame which started to lick the tapestries and hangings in the hallway.
Perry tore down a curtain and wrapped Shivaughn in it, then picking her up he took her out of the front door.
"Is everyone accounted for?" he shouted; having it confirmed by Manners who seemed to be organising things.
"Can someone get to the stables and let the horses out; with the exception of my greys; perhaps you could harness them in the gig and bring it round to the front; I must get my wife to a doctor!"
"Under no circumstances try to save the house, as you may well get hurt in the process; I will get help from the village as soon as I get there and arrange for lodgings for all of you as soon as possible!"
With that he tenderly placed Shivaughn in the gig, climbed in; whipped up the horses and raced away down the drive.

CHAPTER FIFTEEN

Shivaugn came slowly out of the drug induced sleep, the colour returning to her cheeks; the doctor turned to Perry and said; "please do not tax her too long sir, sleep is the best medicine at the moment."
Perry held her hand and said; "thank God you are alive; I could not bear the thought of losing you my dear girl!"
She smiled weakly and murmured; "was it all a bad dream; that awful man, what happened?"
"I will tell you all about it when you have rested;" Perry replied bending to kiss her cheek.
Turning to the doctor he asked anxiously; "is she going to be alright doctor?"
"Of course," the doctor replied, "she's young and healthy, my only concern was for the baby; but there have been no signs that she will miscarry!"
"When she was sufficiently recovered they were invited by the Grimshaws to stay at the vicarage whilst Perry found somewhere permanent to live.
He had ensured that all his staff had been found lodgings in or near the village and assured them of a place when he was settled.
Manners asked him if he had considered rebuilding the Manor and Perry remarked wryly that he never wanted to set eyes on the accurse place again!
"It has too many terrible associations for both my wife and myself for us ever to live happily there again; no it must be a fresh start!"

CHAPTER SIXTEEN

The fire had utterly gutted the Manor and it was silhouetted against the sky like the skeletal remains of some prehistoric beast; gradually over the years it became overgrown and forgotten; the moat gradually dried up and the wood remained untended, becoming the haunt of wild creatures.
The Coombes purchased a splendid Palladian house set in a large park near Aylsham and lived a long and happy life with four children and all the trappings of local gentry. Perry became a Justice of the Peace and was well respected within the local community.
His father in law relented and visited his grandchildren when he could get away from his commitments in Jamaica and the house was full of happiness and contentment.

It is said by the old folk who remember; that on certain nights when the moon is full and the autumn mists swirl around the ruins of Molesly Manor; it would not do to be abroad in Sir Humphrey's Wood otherwise you could be confronted by the wraith of the Moor searching for the Philosopher's Stone amongst the ivy covered rubble!

THE END

THE HOUSE ON THE CLIFF

CHAPTER ONE

My name is Lawrence Alderney and I run a family business in Stepney; as a matter of fact a small solicitor's practice which has seen three generations of Alderneys at the helm.
We deal mainly in conveyancing and probate matters to do with the transfers and disposal of small estates.
One day a strange looking fellow was ushered into my office; he was sporting mutton chop whiskers and had the look of a seafarer about him.
I bade him sit down and rang for coffee, which he took black and drank it noisily from the saucer!
It transpired that he was a sea captain, name of Blackett; he told me that he had travelled the world, but spent most of his time in windjammers bringing tea from China to Wapping!
As he spoke I could not help noticing that his weather beaten face had a haunted look about it and he continually glanced behind him as if he expected to see something there.

He had been born in Norfolk; but for some reason that he would not disclose seemed loathe to return to that County where he owned a property!
"Cliff House be its name; in the village of Haiston;" he stated, "that used to be the Coast Guard house years ago, but it fell into ruin after the lighthouse were built!"
"My father bought the old place and restored it and it has been in the family ever since."
"Why do you wish to sell it?" I enquired.
"Because I wish to retire in London as that is always the place I returned to from the sea sir;" he replied.

Perhaps it was my imagination, but as he spoke a shudder seemed to convulse his person!
Recovering he continued; "I wish the house to be sold as soon as possible and therefore I am prepared to accept any reasonable offer!"
While he was talking I could not help wondering why he had not placed the property in the hands of a local Estate agent that would have been the logical thing to do.
I asked him the question and he became evasive; mumbling something about local superstitions and prejudices!

"Do you wish us to handle the sale for you?" I asked.
His manner brightened and he leaned forward and grasped my hand saying; "That I do sir; you will be doin' me a great service by disposing of it!"
A plan had been formulating in my mind during the conversation and I suggested that I drive up to Haiston and inspect the house.
The fact of the matter was that I had not had a holiday for the last three years due to pressure of work and a few days by the sea would be most acceptable!
"That 'ud be just fine sir;" he cried grasping my hand yet again; "I will leave the address where you can contact me to finalize the sale!"
With that he had a final look around the room and bade me good day!
I sat rather shaken by this odd encounter, wondering what mystery awaited me at Cliff House.

CHAPTER TWO

The journey up to Norfolk was a pleasure, it was early June and the countryside was in full bloom; every thing was fresh and new.
The sun shone brightly as I sped along the London to Newmarket road in my Sunbeam Talbot.
I lunched in Newmarket and then continued towards Norwich; a beautiful cathedral city built around the river Yare.
Then on to North Walsham, a small market town with a large church which had suffered extreme damage to the tower!
Finally by means of a series of meandering byways I joined the coastal road and found the signpost to Haiston.
All this time I was aware that the atmosphere was changing; becoming brooding and almost hostile.
A sea mist was coming inland, creeping across the fields and engulfing the young corn as it came!
Suddenly a figure appeared out of the mist riding a bicycle; I had to swerve and brake violently to avoid running him down.
I wound down the window and enquired as to the whereabouts of Cliff House and received a long stare from the fellow before he replied.
"What you want to be a goin' there for?" he asked suspiciously.
"Because my good man I have been asked to inspect it for a client;" I replied rather shortly.
"Waal I wouldn't goo there if I were you; there are odd goin's on there after dark; people hereabouts don't have nothin' to do wi' it!"
"That is as maybe; but I have to carry out my instructions despite local superstitions!" I retorted.

He reluctantly gave me directions; then mounting his bicycle he disappeared into the mist!

I drove slowly down the road as by now the mist was quite dense and visibility was extremely limited.
I managed to find the turning he had spoken of and gingerly crept along what was a narrow track bordered by a yew hedge.
The mist seemed to cling to the car, extending wispy tendrils around the windscreen as the hypnotic movement of the wipers went back and forth!
A white gate loomed out of the gloom and I left the car and carrying my suitcase I opened the gate; the hinges creaked loudly as I closed it behind me and walked down a long winding path to the house.
I could hear the booming of the breakers on the foreshore as I approached the front door; they seemed very close!
The key was in the place that Blackett had indicated; under a flower pot in the porch and I unlocked the door and walked into the hall.
Within the house the silence was unnerving; almost as if the house was holding its breath awaiting some malevolent happening!
I began to feel that perhaps I had been unwise to accept this commission; but my sense of duty overcame my fear and I found a packet of candles, lit one and carried the rest of the box into the living room.
Setting the candle on the mantelpiece I eventually found an oil lamp, which I lit and stood on the table.
The room now took on a more homely aspect and I went into the pantry to see what was available.
There were several tins of soup and one of corned beef which I opened and ate together with a couple of rounds of bread from a loaf that I had purchased in Norwich.

Having satisfied the inner man I went upstairs to examine the bedrooms which were spacious and looked over the cliffs out to sea.
A white light suddenly swept across the window illuminating the room and I remembered the light house that Blackett had spoken of!
I could just see the beach as by now the mist had disappeared as quickly as it had come and the moon was tracing a brilliant pathway across the sea towards the shore.
My eye was caught by a figure moving in the moonlight across the beach towards the cliffs; there was something disturbing about the way it moved; almost a sinuous, but determined gait!
Must be a fisherman I thought, tending his nets perhaps before putting out to sea?
However there lurked a growing doubt in the back of my mind that what I had observed was perhaps not human!

CHAPTER THREE

I made myself a drink and selecting the smaller of the two bedrooms turned in for the night.
I awoke the next morning with the sun streaming through the window and the sound of the gentle surge of the sea.
So much for superstitious nonsense I thought and went downstairs to perform my ablutions and have some breakfast.
On entering the kitchen the smell of seaweed assailed my nostrils and I noticed a trail of watery marks going towards the door!
Mystified I opened the back door which led out into an orchard of gnarled ancient fruit trees; all leaning away from sea, presumably due to the prevailing winds?
A path led to the edge of the cliff where steps had been cut leading down to the beach.
As I looked down the tide was coming in; however where the beach was clear there were similar marks going towards the tide line that I had seen in the kitchen!

Somewhat apprehensive I returned to the house and started to prepare breakfast; I had just sat down when there came a knock at the back door; answering it I was confronted by a fisherman carrying a pail.
"Mornin' to ye sir;" he cried, "I've just landed these here silver darlins' this mornin' they are as fresh as kecksies; would ye be wantin' some for your dinner?"
I bought half a dozen as he chattered on.
"Have ye just moved in sir?" he asked, only the old place has been empty for years; I didn't know it had been sold!"
I told him that I was up from London for a few days; he nodded sagely and added; "don't you teark no notice of

any tales you might hear in the village; they're all a bit leery if ye ask me!" he made a circular motion with his finger beside his head.
Then with a cheery wave he was on his way along the cliff top towards the lighthouse.
It dawned on me afterwards that he had no means of knowing that there were in fact any occupants at Cliff House!
I had arrived in the mist and only been out this morning; then I thought perhaps he had seen me standing on the cliff from his boat!
I could have sworn that I had seen no boat, either at sea or on the foreshore; I put the matter out of my mind as I cleared the table and began preparing the herrings for lunch.
Finishing this task I decided to work up an appetite by walking along the beach; the tide was going out when I reached the bottom of the steps and I commenced to walk along the smooth sand at the water's edge.
I noticed how the water oozed out of the sand each time my foot was placed on it leaving a partial foot print ready to be obliterated when the tide came back in!
For some reason I felt I was being watched; however when I turned quickly to scan the shore behind me and the top of the cliffs, there was nothing but the sea birds with their strange cries skimming the waves and wheeling overhead!
A feeling of extreme isolation stole over me as I walked along the lonely shore and a desire for companionship welled up inside me.

CHAPTER FOUR

After returning to the house and having a plate of fried herring, which were excellent and as fresh as the fisherman claimed, I decided to do some work and measured up the rooms; searching for damp and all the other tasks to do with checking a property before sale! I became so engrossed with my duties that I lost all sense of time and suddenly realised the sun had begun to set!
I left for the village which seemed further than I had thought; coming eventually to a forbidding Norman church set on a hill.
Then into a straggling street full of old cottages and a thatched pub with a sign outside proclaiming The Fisherman's Rest.

There was soft light emanating from the mullioned windows and the strains of a concertina playing an old ballad.
As I entered the bar I was aware of a scene of a low, beamed room full of tobacco smoke populated by an assortment of fishermen and farm labourers in earnest conversation, about what I knew not!
Walking across the sawdust covered floor to the bar I was suddenly aware that the room had fallen silent; I was the focus of attention!
The landlord; a great brute of a fellow sporting a drooping moustache watched me with an air of detachment as he polished a glass tankard carefully then placed it on the counter.
"What can I get for you sir;" he said; I did not like the emphasis that he had put on sir; it was almost a sneer!
"A pint of bitter if you please landlord," I replied.
"Best or this;" he gestured towards a pump with a brand I had never heard of!
"Best Please;" I said.

"You are not from these parts are you sir;" there it was again that emphasis!
"No I am not!"
He grunted triumphantly and nodded to the listening audience; then proceeded to pull a pint of his 'Best.
I sipped it and decided that if this was his best, I hated to think what his worst was like!

"You on holiday hereabouts?" he said quizzically.
"No, as a matter of fact I am staying at Cliff House for a few days;" I replied.
It was as if someone had just died; there was a sudden mutual intake of breath, then the murmuring started.
One of the fishermen; a grizzled old salt, looked hard at me and said; "don't you know that there plairce is haunted?"
"No I don't;" I said angrily, "what's more I don't believe in all the superstitious nonsense I've been hearing since I arrived!"
"You would be well advised to leave that accursed house before ye see somethin' ye'll never fergit;" he retorted.
By this time I was very irritated by the claustrophobic atmosphere of this place; so I drank up and walked into the night without a backward glance!
The moon was up by this time and lit up the road as I walked along; casting strange shadows, including mine on the way.
What an awful place this was; what people; why are they obsessed with the supernatural and what is there to fear in Cliff House?
These thoughts filled my mind as I walked down the path towards the house; as I approached the windows seemed like sightless eyes gazing blankly at me as I neared the door.

CHAPTER FIVE

I turned in early and had not been asleep long when I was suddenly awake and listening.
There came a long unearthly cry dying away in a despairing scream; it seemed to come from the rear of the house; I felt the hair on the back of my head stand up!
I arose and went to the window; the moon was again lighting up a pathway across the sea; but I could perceive nothing.
I stayed by the window for a long time, but nothing else happened and I returned to bed.
Next morning I awoke with a start; there was that damned smell again; seaweed, but this time there was another odour, a sweet sickly smell, which try as I might, I could not place!
I dressed hurriedly and went down to the shore; walking briskly along in the bright sunshine my spirits rose and my mind turned to other things.
I would soon have to wind up my little sojourn by the sea and return to London; as by now I had all the information I required about the house; at least the physical aspect of it!

I risked another visit to the village for provisions and called into the local Post Office where I was served by a severe looking woman who obviously did not approve of strangers!
There were one or two customers hovering in the background and I could feel their eyes boring into my back.
I was glad to return to Cliff House where I lit the stove and cooked myself a meal; washing it down with a bottle of wine I had bought at the shop!

Then down to the shore again where I found the fisherman collecting his nets.

"Hello sir; takin' a constitutional?" he said.

"You could say that;" I replied, to tell you the truth I shall not be sorry to leave tomorrow, this place gives me the creeps!"

"Doant tell me the locals hev got to ye?" he said with a chuckle.

"As a matter of fact I don't think I've ever met such a parochial, suspicious, unfriendly bunch in my life;" I said bitterly!"

"Waal I did warn ye;" he said, "the trouble hereabouts is to do with history!"

"What do you mean?" I said blankly.

He put down his nets and took out a little clay pipe, tamped it with some tobacco, lit it and puffed contentedly for a while.

"Many years ago, he began; this village were desperately poor and relied on wreckin' for survival. Many a fine vessel was lured onto the shoals out yonder;" he gestured with his thumb; "and they was helped there by 'false lights' onshore!"

"They didn't stop at takin' the cargo; they killed anyone who got to the shore and took anythin' of value they had!"

"The place got such an evil reputation that a Coast Guard house was built to put a stop to it."

However some of the officers started to disappear in mysterious circumstances and eventually the place had to be closed as no one local would man it!"

"Oh, come on that's stretching things a little isn't it?" I said in disbelief..

His face changed suddenly from the jolly tar he was normally and he looked gravely at me and said; "there are things about the sea sir that shouldn't be scoffed at; a man does so at his peril!"

"Anyway I must be a goin'; soon be high tide and I'll be puttin' out to catch some more silver darlins'.
"Fare you well sir and a safe journey home tomorrow!"
I watched him as he strode along the tide line towards where his boat was drawn up on the foreshore and turned towards the house reflecting on the extraordinary story he had just told me

.CHAPTER SIX

The moon was full that night and whether it was the brightness of it or my restless mind continually turning over what the fisherman had told me; I could not get to sleep, constantly turning in bed to get comfortable! Eventually I drifted off into a troubled sleep; seeming to hear that cry again, far away.

I was wide awake and terrified; the moon lit up the room casting shadows on the walls; but my eyes were drawn to a figure crouching at the foot of my bed!
It was of human shape, just; but there the resemblance ended.
I looked on in horror as I took in the awful appearance of it.
The head had been a skull; but now every part that had been flesh was covered in molluscs ranging from barnacles to mussels; the eye sockets were inhabited by marine worms which oozed out of the nostrils.
The scalp was covered in seaweed which hung down like an obscene wig and the smell; oh that smell, it will live with me to the grave!
Now I knew what that other smell was; that sweet sickly stench; it was decaying flesh!
The thing seemed to be clad in rotting seaman's garb of an age long since gone and it crouched there motionless, staring at me with those sightless eyes.
The thing and I sat face to face for what seemed like an eternity; then my nerve broke and I began screaming; I could not stop screaming until mercifully I lost consciousness!

I awoke in a bright, white decorated room in a metal bed; there was a cabinet beside it with a vase full of daffodils on it!

Daffodils? but surely it is May; on endeavouring to rise to my horror I found that I was held by restraints; what has happened to me?

Just then a cheery nurse came into the room and said; "Hello, awake at last?"

"What has happened and where am I?" I asked.

"All in good time;" she said leaning over the bed and injecting my left arm.

"There, that will help you to sleep;" she said.

"But I've only just woken up!" I said weakly as I slipped into the arms of Morpheus once more!

Some time later, I don't know how long; the doctor came in to see me; a tall thin gangling fellow in a white coat; he sat on the bed and asked me how I felt!

"I'm confused, where am I and how long have I been here?" I groaned.

He smiled and said; "It's early days yet; you have been through a terrible trauma of some kind and need plenty of rest.

It began to come back to me then; the thing at the bottom of my bed; I began looking round the room to see if it had gone!

Every time I awoke I checked to see if it was about and I could swear that now and again something just at the margin of my sight moved; but when I turned to look it had gone.

Summer has come and gone now and the leaves are falling outside my barred window and still Doctor Hennesy says that I am not quite ready for the outside world.

Sometimes when I feel particularly depressed I am aware of the smell of seaweed emanating from the corner of the room.
Please God; don't let me see it again!

                                                    THE END

PUSSYKINS

CHAPTER ONE

   I hate that cat! It glares at me with those baleful green eyes every time we meet and spits at me whilst the fur on its back stands on end.
What it thinks I have done to it I cannot imagine, but it's very upsetting nevertheless.
On the other hand it positively squirms with pleasure when on my wife's lap; purring loudly and allowing its tum' to be tickled!
I tried that once and finished up having stitches in my hand; it just licked its lips and stalked triumphantly out of the room.
We live in a small village near the coast where we settled once I had retired; it is fairly typical of its type, filled mainly with good old country characters like Stockbrokers, Bankers and various other Professional people!
Where the original inhabitants have gone to God alone knows as they certainly couldn't afford to live here any more!
That is apart from the Post Mistress; heaven knows how old she is; I think she may be related to Methusela!
I can see her now stamping documents with almost homicidal pleasure; with her remaining hair scraped back on the nape of her neck and her protruding two front teeth holding up her top lip, dispensing endless advice to all who would listen in that high pitched cracked voice of hers.

I blame her for my persecution by Pussykins, it was she who persuaded my wife to bring him into the house.

Anne had called in to the Post Office to buy some stamps and immediately Miss Flowerdew fixed her with that basilisk eye of hers and said; "you look just like the sort of person who would take in a poor little pussy cat!"

Before my wife could protest the old besom had produced a wicker basket containing three little bundles of fur attended by an anxious mother cat.

"There you are my dear," she cooed, "just have a look at these little dears, melts your heart doesn't it?"

Anne found herself outside the shop with one of the kittens in a carrier bag and no stamps!

The animal immediately took over the household and most of my wife's time; I now began to fall over bowls of cat food and water placed in obscure places in the kitchen and being hissed at on every occasion!

The thing seemed to grow at an alarming rate, consuming huge mounds of meat and fish; with Pussykins about the 5000 would have had no chance!

He would then totter off into the lounge and sleep it off in front of the wood burner, snoring hard enough to make the windows rattle!

Not content with this he began a reign of terror on the garden birds, despatching them at an alarming rate.

I did my best to discourage him, even fitting a bell on his collar; I got scratched for that too!

Anne drew the line at the bell; saying that it was cruel and horrid of me to do such a thing; things were a bit strained between us after that.

I found myself spending more time on the golf course just to keep out of Pussykins way and that didn't suit either!

"You should take your niblicks or whatever you call them and go and sleep in the club house;" she said, "I hardly ever see you now anyway.
The cat was curled up on her lap and opened one eye; on perceiving me he managed a faint hiss and then went back to sleep!

CHAPTER TWO

Things went from bad to worse with our relationship and I started to feel that the cat had taken my place in the pecking order of the household.
The last straw as far as I was concerned was finding that he was now allowed to sleep on our bed!
I voiced my displeasure in no uncertain terms and was given a tongue lashing by Anne about always having resented poor Pussykins and being nasty to him etc. etc. and that if I didn't like it there was always the Golf Club!
Well; I lost it big time at that and grabbing the cat I threw him out of the back door and shut it firmly!
"It's him or me," I shouted; my wife's response was to throw a suitcase at me and indicate that I should leave.
That brought me to my senses; I couldn't afford to take up permanent residence elsewhere; so I elected to eat a large portion of Humble Pie!

After that I found myself relegated to Dogsbody Second Class doing all the menial chores including feeding the cat!
I began to think of devious ways of spiking his milk; introducing noxious substances into his cat food or braining him with a spade; but I just couldn't bring myself to it somehow.
Meanwhile he grew fatter and more insufferable every day; registering his loathing of me at every opportunity!

Then Fate took a hand in the situation; he got run over outside the house by the local milkman!
The poor man was most apologetic, reverently carrying the large limp body and carefully setting it down on the doorstep.

"I hope this won't affect my deliverin' the milk," he said earnestly; "I shall miss bringin' him his Gold Top every day!"

Seeing Anne about to set about him I hurriedly intervened; shaking him gratefully by the hand as I escorted him hurriedly off the premises.

I dug a deep hole joyously in the orchard and lowered Pussykin's transparent carrier with him lying in state inside.

Anne insisted that I make a wooden cross to mark the grave and laid a large bouquet of flowers on the site.

It was a long hard winter that year and when Spring eventually showed up I decided to do some pruning in the orchard.

You can imagine my surprise when I found Pussykin's grave open and no sign of him!

The hair on the back of my neck rose as I also noticed that the cross had been broken in two and thrown to one side.

What diabolical work was this or had he indeed risen from the dead!

That would be too much to bear, having a phantom cat roaming the neighbourhood.

I looked carefully at the ground around the grave; there were no animal tracks or other signs of a predator having done the deed, he had literally vanished from the face of the earth!

CHAPTER THREE

I shivered involuntarily and a wave of foreboding ran through me; this cannot be happening I thought; but a further look at the scene confirmed my worst fears, not only that but I was going to have to break the news to Anne!
She didn't take the news well; after the initial sobbing and wailing had subsided she looked at me suspiciously and said; "What have you done with him?"
I protested my innocence, but she would have none of it saying; "you always hated that poor cat, you've done something horrible with him haven't you?"
Despite all my protestations I was relegated to the spare room and the golf course for a crime I had not committed!
It was about that time that George, my golfing partner disappeared; the police made a search of the surrounding countryside and dragged the river without success!
There were rumours in the clubhouse amongst some of the chaps about an extra marital affair, but nothing was ever proved.
Then a month later Ralph, a retired accountant friend also went missing; he had gone to visit his mother who lived nearby, but never arrived!
His car was found abandoned in a copse some time later; there were no signs of a struggle or traces of blood and Forensics only found the prints belonging to him and his wife in the car.
The police were baffled, they could find no motive for the disappearance and despite full media coverage nothing came to light!

Anne played Bridge with the two wives every Wednesday and during one of her rare civil moments she remarked to me that each of them had been given one of the kittens from the litter that Pussykins had come from!

My mind homed in on this chance remark; there had to be some significant fact here; but for the life of me I couldn't think of what it could be!

Then it hit me: an idea so bizarre that I dare not discuss it with anyone as they would certainly think that I had lost my marbles!

In some way not yet clear Miss Flowerdew was involved in the disappearances of my two friends and I was going to get to the bottom of it.

I called round to see the wives and asked some pertinent questions about the movements of the two men on the days they went missing.

It transpired that both had a reason to call at the Post Office; for what purpose the wives did not know; except that their spouses had both mentioned it!

I came away convinced that therein lay the reason (however obscure) ,for their disappearances.

I began to observe Miss Flowerdew's movements and destinations each day and found that she was a creature of habit.

Mondays were usually Pension day, so she spent all day in the shop; Tuesday also kept her busy as the wholesaler came with stock for the shop!

The only days she absented herself were Wednesdays and Fridays, leaving her assistant Muriel in charge whilst Miss Flowerdew tripped off to the church.

I followed her at a discreet distance through the churchyard and hid myself at the back of the Nave observing her movements!

She and another equally gaunt woman were polishing the brasses and arranging the flowers whilst communing in low voices, much to my irritation.

From the snatches I was able to hear they seemed to be discussing some forthcoming event; however despite all my efforts I was unable to glean further information!

As they departed, from my vantage point I observed a sheet of paper flutter out of the gaunt woman's bag! Eagerly I pounced and hurriedly stuffed the missive into my coat pocket; on arriving home I went into my study and eagerly read the note.

CHAPTER FOUR

    As I read the spidery scrawl my mouth dropped open; I could hardly believe what I was looking at.
They were planning a celebration of the Witches Sabbath on Walpurgis Night!
I had read a number of books on Black Magic when young; eventually concluding that it was just an excuse to indulge in ceremonial orgies!
They were both a bit up the tooth for such frolics and I couldn't suppress a small titter at the picture it conjured up in my mind!
However I resolved to follow them to where the ceremony was to take place as they had not mentioned the location in the note.
I did not reveal my plan to anyone in case they decided that I was a suitable candidate for the Booby Hatch!
I impatiently counted off the days until finally it arrived; packing some sandwiches and a steel thermos flask of coffee in the car I set off to shadow Miss Flowerdew!

    Sure enough at 18-30 hours a large black limmo' with blacked out window crept up to the Post Office, out came Miss Flowerdew carrying a small suitcase, she climbed into the back of the limmo' and they were off.
I kept at a safe distance behind them and soon we were on the A11.heading for Thetford, then turning off to Grimes Graves (a Neolithic flint mining area)!
However we turned off onto a dirt road and continued down to a plantation of fir trees where there was a large derelict house.
There the limmo' stopped and I hastily pulled the car into the entrance to a logging road, I would have to continue on foot.

Stuffing the sandwiches and flask in the ample pockets of my waterproof, I slung my binoculars over my shoulder and set off through the trees.
As I neared the house I spotted a couple of 'heavies' standing by the limmo' they looked capable of dealing with any intruders.
The rest of the coven seemed to have gone into the house; probably to get changed into their ceremonial garb.

Sure enough after a few minutes the witches trooped out wearing long black robes with hoods.
Then a figure swaggered out of the house wearing a blood red robe covered in black cabalistic signs carrying a sword and a wand of iron; it was Miss Flowerdew!
All the others bowed as she went to the head of the procession and led them into the forest.

CHAPTER FIVE

I carefully circled round the house to avoid being spotted by the two guards and picked up the coven making their way down a narrow path.
Eventually they came out into a large clearing in the centre of which stood an altar covered in a black cloth covered in signs of the zodiac!
At one end there was a canopy over a table covered in what looked like leather bound books and a large bowl with a long curved knife lying beside it!
Aha! I thought that will be for the sacrificial cockerel I expect; how wrong I was!
The ceremony began with chanting which seemed to go on interminably; Miss Flowerdew however seemed to be referring to various books and making signs with the wand, eventually she turned to the worshipers and raised her arms; the chanting stopped.
In her thin reedy voice she addressed them; there was something unearthly about her; she seemed to be surrounded by a powerful aura and her eyes blazed triumphantly as she spoke!
"It is my pleasant duty to welcome you brothers and sisters in the Craft to this celebration of our Master's power!"

"This year my divinations have indicated that power is going to be magnified by a third sacrifice and to show his gratitude our Master is sending his representative to take part in the ceremony!"
There was a collective sigh of appreciation from the crowd as she continued; "we have had our tribulations however with unbelievers and those who would interfere with our Work!"
Here she stopped and turned to where I was hiding; looking straight at me she pointed her wand, "there is

the one who would dare to try and destroy us; seize him!"

I turned to escape only to run straight into the burly arms of the two guards who had come silently up behind me!

I struggled violently, but to no avail and they soon had me trussed up like a chicken; then they carried me shoulder high towards the altar.

"You see my brothers and sisters," she shrieked, our Master has sent us the third sacrificed bearing out my predictions!"

"Ready this pitiful specimen for sacrifice," she commanded; the men did as they were bid and I was secured by leather straps to the altar.

I gazed wildly around for some means of escape; but it was hopeless I was doomed; my mind became a blank with fear and despair!

She advanced towards me holding the curved knife in one hand and the bowl in the other chanting as she came.

I could see her face in the moonlight; it was the face of a mad woman; she seemed to be in some sort of ecstatic trance!

She stopped beside the altar still chanting then suddenly stopped and pointed a bony finger to a spot behind the crowd; "See, see He comes, the promised one, coming to share in our celebrations!"

Everyone turned to look and then they all prostrated themselves before whatever it was.

I couldn't see anything at first; thinking that they must all be on drugs or something.

Then something large and covered in fur sprang effortlessly onto the altar beside me!

CHAPTER SIX

Its red eyes blazed triumphantly as it gazed at me; the smell of rotting flesh assaulted my nostrils only to be replaced by its foetid breath as it moved closer; it was Pussykins!
I nearly passed out, but the mad old witch raised the knife above her head and it flashed in the moonlight as it came down and plunged deep into my arm.
I screamed with pain as the blood flowed and Miss Flowerdew collected it in the sacrificial bowl.
She held the bowl above her head as she recited some sort of ritual; then turning to the crowd she called on them to stand and observe.
Lowering the bowl she reverently placed it before the hideous creature who sniffed it then began to lap noisily! A drum started to beat out a rhythm and the coven divested themselves of their robes and joining hands began to dance in a great circle around the altar. Faster and faster the drum beat out and the circle became faster too; I turned just in time to see the glittering blade sweeping down in a great arc towards my chest and lost consciousness!

I awoke with a start sitting in my armchair in the lounge; "thank goodness you're awake; I thought you were having a heart attack; shouting and mumbling, poor Pussykins ran out of the room with fright!"
The wife continued; "now you're back in the land of the living we could do with some more logs; the wood burner needs building up."
As I went out to the woodshed I saw the damned cat stalking a blackbird and shouted at it; it glared at me and slunk away.
I hate that cat!

THE END

THE WATCHER

CHAPTER ONE

Anthony Delusignan was a bitter man; last of his line through injudicious investment in the Stock Market; gambling debts and two extravagant marriages; he had been forced to sell the family Estate and most of it's contents; finally finishing up in one of the gate houses on it's periphery!
As he gazed moodily down the field at the back of his dwelling thinking of his failing fortunes his eye was caught by a motionless figure standing by the gate at the bottom of the field; it appeared to be staring at the window where he stood!
It was hard to make out detail at that distance; but it appeared to be a man dressed in moleskin breeches' leggings and short top boots; on closer scrutiny there seemed to be a Collie dog lying at the man's feet.
The figure remained motionless as Anthony gazed; intrigued he turned to pick up his spy glass from the small table behind him.
Raising the glass to his eye he focussed it in the direction of the far end of the field where the figure stood.
To his astonishment it was no longer there!
Frantically he swept the whole area with his glass, but to no avail; the man and his dog were gone.
"Damned poachers," he muttered angrily; "we knew how to deal with them in the old days!"
He was a large man with a florid face and a large paunch; a tribute to his liking for rich food and great quantities of drink!

He also had an irascible manner which many of his erstwhile tenants had been subjected to.
The Delusignans had come over with the Conqueror and like many of their noble contemporaries had feathered their nests to the detriment of their Saxon tenants.
It would be fair to say that there was little love lost between them and a sort of hostile acceptance was as good as it got!
He poured himself a stiff whisky still harping on about 'damned poachers', musing, "we would have put the man traps out in the woods for 'em; too soft nowadays; give 'em the option of laying up with a broken leg or bein' brought before the Bench; where I could send 'em to Botany Bay, What?"
Feeling somewhat buoyed up by this imaginary triumph he poured another whisky and carried it through to the kitchen to see what was happening about his luncheon.
His housekeeper, Mrs. Neave, was not there; neither was there anything cooking; the stove was cold and nothing had been prepared!
"Damned unreliable old biddy;" he swore; what in Hell am I goin' to eat?"

  He went into the pantry and managed to find some cheese and a stale loaf; cutting off a large piece of cheese and a doorstep of bread he picked up his drink and went back into the study.
He slept badly that night despite the amount of whisky he had consumed and in the small hours he lay awake thinking of the strange figure he had seen at the bottom of the field; there had been something menacing in the figure's stillness and unnerving about the way it had disappeared, almost as if it had ceased to exist!

Delusignan shivered; feeling a sudden chill he decided to rise and make himself a dish of tea.

Whilst relighting the stove he heard a shrill whistle from outside; crossing to the window he drew the curtains and looked out.

Dawn was just breaking and a pall of white mist hung over the fields: some sheep had been turned out at the rear of the cottage and were milling around as if something was trying to round them up; but he could see neither shepherd nor dog!

He quickly drew the curtains closed and when the kettle finally boiled he had his tea and went back to bed.

CHAPTER TWO

   He awoke with a start feeling that all was not well; on consulting his watch found that it was ten thirty of the clock!
"Damn; I should have been up early this mornin;" there was a Point to Point at the Fakenham race course that day and he liked to have a flutter and a few drinks with his cronies; that is when he could afford it!
Fortunately his allowance had come from his lawyer Fenwick yesterday, so he was in funds for a while at least.
When the Estate had finally been wound up there had been a modest residual sum left which Fenwick had persuaded him to invest in a small annuity.
It was by no means a fortune, but it just about kept him solvent if he was careful!

   He shaved and dressed hurriedly and went out to the stable behind the cottage where he quickly tacked up his old gelding and set off at a smart trot towards the Fakenham road.
By now the sun was up and there were the makings of a fine day; "goin' should be firm today," he thought as he jogged along; "if Belerephon is runnin' I'll have five guineas on the blighter!"
And so he did and the horse won at five to one, which put Anthony in a triumphant mood; he bought his friends dinner at the Crown Hotel and drinks a plenty!
Replete and rather the worse for wear he found himself trotting homewards a little after twelve of the clock on a clear, crisp night with a full moon following him silently behind the branches of the tree lined road.
Suddenly his horse threw up it's head and tried to bolt; with difficulty he managed to regain control, swearing

at the frightened beast and looking nervously around him to see what had been the cause of it's fright!

   At first he could see nothing; but then his eye was caught by what looked like a figure standing motionless under a group of oak trees by the road.
Fearing an ambush by footpads he drew his horse pistol from the saddle holster; stood up in his stirrups and bellowed; "come on out where I can see you!"
There was no response; so he shouted, "I shall count to three and if you are not out in the open I shall shoot;" there was deathly silence, his nerve failed him and he fired!
Quickly reloading his pistol he urged his horse forward towards the trees, every nerve fibre tingling with apprehension.
Just then the moonlight chased away the shadows under the trees; there was nothing, apart from a white gash in the bark where the ball had struck!
"Must have been a trick of the light;" he muttered; could have sworn there was someone there."
He continued on his way finding himself continually on edge, shooting glances at every possible piece of cover en route!
He finally arrived home feeling drained and consumed a large brandy before retiring to his bed.

   He was running down an endless dark lane being pursued by some dreadful unknown being; he could hear its relentless padding steps keeping pace with his stumbling flight.
He dared not look round as he instinctively knew that the sight of whatever it was that pursued him would cause his legs to give out and it would be upon him!
Meanwhile there was a pain in his chest and down his left arm growing ever more fierce.

The thing, whatever it was seemed to be gaining on him until he could actually feel its foul breath on the back of his neck; then he was falling, falling in an endless parabola through total darkness!
He awoke with a start, covered in sweat and the bedclothes were strewn across the floor; sunlight was streaming through the window and when he consulted his watch it was again half past ten of the clock!

   Sounds of movement were coming from the kitchen and in view of last night's experience he recovered his old cavalry sabre from under the bed and dressed in his night attire flung open the kitchen door only to discover a startled Mrs.Neave!
"Decided to come back have ye?" he snarled
Straightening up Mrs Neave snapped back; "I have been down with the ague this last three days sir; not that I'd expect any sympathy from you!"
She seemed totally unafraid of him and always gave as good as she got; probably safe in the knowledge that no one else in the village would 'do' for him anyway!
"I suppose you would like some breakfast;" she said sardonically.
"No," he said, I will have a bite of lunch when I return!"
Without further explanation he shaved and dressed and went out.

CHAPTER THREE

   The local doctor lived in a large Georgian house on the edge of the village; it had at one time belonged to the mistress of one of Anthony's predecessors; but on their untimely demise she had collected any monies due to her, packed her bags and caught the stage to London.
Where no doubt the pickings were much better for a lady of her considerable talents!
Anthony Delusignan strode into the hall and threw down his hat on the table and shouted; "are ye about Doctor?"
A small rather dapper man came quickly out of his consulting room to greet him; Doctor White had a full head of grey hair, a pleasant face and immaculately manicured hands which he extended in a welcoming gesture.
"What can I do for you sir on this fine morning?"
"Not sleepin' very well," responded the Captain; "bit nervy to tell ye the truth!"

   "Step into my consulting room sir; step behind the screen and remove your upper garments so that I may examine you."
"Is that really necessary;" grumbled Anthony; "got a busy day d'ye see?"
"Sir if I am going to help you a physical examination is necessary;" the good doctor replied.
The reluctant patient complied with the doctor's request, still grumbling; on examining him the doctor looked grave!
Taking a long time sounding his chest back and front, he looked in his eyes and mouth, finally telling him to get dressed.
"Well, what's the verdict Doctor?" he asked nervously.

Doctor White bent his head for a moment then looked him directly in the eye and said; "I am warning you that unless you drastically reduce your intake of drink it will be the end of you!"
"You have had a heart attack recently and unless you take my advice you may well have a more serious one or even a seizure!"

Anthony was taken aback by the Doctors candour; "don't pull yer punches do ye Doctor?"
"I have known you for many years Anthony;" said Doctor White, "and I am sure you would rather hear the truth!"
"Yes; I suppose I would, but even so it has come as a bit of a shock; ye see I rely on a drink or two at night to get me off to sleep Doctor."
"Not sleeping well eh? Well don't worry I can give you some laudanum for that; just wait there and I will make you up a prescription."
The doctor returned with a small green bottle containing some brownish liquid;
"take it last thing at night in the dose shown on the bottle; under no circumstances exceed the prescribed amount!"
Thanking the doctor Anthony stumbled out into the sunlight a very chastened man!
"One foot in the grave by Jove," he muttered to himself, "have to cut down on me social life; God what a prospect!"
He hardly remembered getting home, being so preoccupied that he nearly walked under the wheels of a passing cart; shaking his fist impotently at the receding back of the driver.
Finally he reached his cottage and the appetising smell of liver and onions assailed his nostrils; reminding him that some degree of normality still remained!

CHAPTER FOUR

During the Peninsular Wars he had bought a commission and joined the Light Cavalry as a Captain. Fighting through Portugal and into Spain where he had been wounded at the battle of Talavera.
It happened just outside the town during a skirmish with French cavalry and he and several of his men were cut down.
He was sent to Lisbon to recuperate and as he regained his strength he began to attend functions where he met Portuguese people of quality.
At one particular function he met a minor official of the Portuguese Embassy, Senhoor da Silva; however he was not the most interesting member of the family as far as Anthony was concerned!
Da Silva had the most ravishing daughter named Magdalena; she was eighteen, precocious with hair as black as a raven's wing; eyes like two dark pools that a man could drown in and she had learned to speak English with an accent that drove him wild!
Needless to say he was soon head over heels in love and determined to take her to wife!

Her father was flattered that a member of the English aristocracy should show an interest in his daughter; particularly since her prospects in Portugal were uncertain, due to the fact that he had no title.
Therefore he cultivated Delusignan's acquaintance and invited him to his home;
a modest villa in Cascais near the Royal Palace.
There the young couple got to know each other on a strictly formal basis; Magdalena being chaperoned by her Duenna at all times!
Things took their course and he finally took the bull by the horns and asked her father for her hand in marriage.

They were married in Lisbon's Manueline cathedral to the sound of the ringing of bells and much celebration, his fellow officers providing a Guard of Honour!
His Colonel granted him extended leave and the happy couple left for their honeymoon in Italy.

CHAPTER FIVE

Delusignan sat at his escritoire writing a letter to his aunt Maude requesting money again: mainly because she was the only member of the family who had been canny enough to hold onto it!
Maude was his father's elder sister and had married well to a Port importer; it was more of a business arrangement than a marriage made in heaven!
Luckily for Maude her husband had the decency to drown in a storm in the Bay of Biscay whilst returning from a visit to his warehouses in Oporto, they had been married for just three years!
She had inherited his entire estate and with the business flourishing and Port being a favourite tipple at that time she did not want for a thing.

The sun was setting outside as he glanced out of the study window; he stiffened in his chair and muttered; "it's there again!"
Sure enough there was the figure of a man standing at the end of the field; strangely the golden light of the sun's rays didn't seem to catch the features of the face which remained obscure.
The man stood motionless looking at Delusignan, who was transfixed' returning its gaze like a rabbit mesmerised by a stoat!
Finally breaking the spell and determined to confront this upstart he rushed to the back door and out into the garden.
The figure was gone; vanished in the few seconds it had taken him to get outside; he climbed over the style into the field and walked down towards where the figure had stood.

There was an iron gate that led into the next field, he went through thinking that the man may have hidden behind the hedge; but there was no sign of him.
Just as he was retracing his step back to the house he heard a shrill whistle from the adjoining wood. Dusk was beginning to fall and there was a sudden chill in the air;
He shivered and decided that discretion was indeed the better part of valour and returned home!

CHAPTER SIX

The happy couple returned from Italy having spent the remainder of their Honeymoon in Rome seeing the sights.
Anthony was looking forward to rejoining his Regiment and reported to Command Headquarters in Oporto.
However he was to receive a nasty shock; he was ordered to take a medical examination in the light of the wounds he had received at Talabera!
The surgeon examined the affected area round his shoulder and back where he had been slashed by the French sabre and stated that he could not recommend a return to combat as there was severe damage to the pectoral muscle.
"Why not?" exclaimed Anthony angrily.
"Simply because I cannot guarantee that your arm won't let you down during action;" replied the surgeon.
"Will I be able to return to active service in a while if I rest?"
The surgeon shrugged; "I cannot say; perhaps in the meantime you could apply for a non combative role."
"Not damned likely;" snorted Anthony; "become a damned scribbler? The Delusignans have always been fightin' stock ever since the Conqueror; it's a bally disgrace!"

The Surgeon stood up; "well there it is; there is nothing more I can do for you, Good day!"
Angry and frustrated he returned to his lodgings and broke the news to Magdalena.
She tried to comfort him; "Ah sweetheart never mind; perhaps it is Kismet and you are meant to do something else."

"I don't know anything else but soldierin,"he retorted and stormed out to get drunk at the officers mess.
This went on for several days until one morning Magdalena sat him down; held his hands and said; "my darling you are destroying yourself and it solves nothing; maybe it is better if we go to your home in England where things may become clearer?"
A look from those sparkling dark eyes convinced him that she was right!
"No good mopin' around here in Portugal I suppose; might as well do as ye say!"
So they packed their things ready for the voyage home; he resigned his commission, said his farewells to his brother officers and they sailed a week later bound for Portsmouth!

CHAPTER SEVEN

Despite the laudanum he still wasn't sleeping well at all, awakening in the small hours and pacing about the house, occasionally peering out of the study window as it grew light!
"Those damned sheep are always dashin' about as if all the devils in hell were after them;" he grumbled, "can't think what gets into the stupid beasts."
He had not seen the figure for some days now, but had heard that sinister whistle from time to time, usually at dusk or just before dawn!
He was finding it hard to do without a drink, he really had tried; recently he had taken to having the odd nip of brandy, 'just to ward off the craving!
He knew this was not the answer; but isolation just emphasised the difficulty of giving up.
What he really needed was something to cheer him up; "I know just the thing;" he exclaimed; "I'll ride over and visit old Turvey; "haven't seen him in an age; keeps a good table and likes a game of cards!"

Sir Leonard Turvey, Bart resided at Madderly Hall a crumbling old moated Grange on the edge of Sutton fen.
The place had a sinister reputation and the locals spoke of young women disappearing from the area from time to time; intimating that it had something to do with the Grange!
However Anthony had no knowledge of these ugly rumours and set out early one Spring morning to visit his old friend.
It was a long journey and he did not arrive until late in the day; riding through the archway into the inner courtyard he dismounted as the late afternoon sun

reflected off the mullioned windows; but there seemed an air of desolation about the place.
He waited, but no servant appeared to take his horse; "this is a rum go," he muttered, "no one to greet a feller after a long ride!"
He tethered his horse to a ring in the wall and walked across the courtyard to the studded main door and tugged at the bell rope.
A doleful clangour came from somewhere in the bowels of the house adding to the eerie atmosphere of the place.
He waited for someone to answer the door, but no one came; "this is damned odd," he said out loud, "I suppose the fella's gone abroad or something!"

"He's dead," the voice came from behind him causing him to spin round and he beheld a short, ferret faced man holding a shotgun under his arm.
"What might your business be?" said the man.
Anthony was furious and snapped back, "none of yours and that's a fact!"
The man smirked slyly and said; "that's where you're wrong; I have been employed to make sure that there are no suspicious characters hanging about the place and that nothing is removed!"
"How dare you speak to me like that;" roared Anthony almost apoplectic with rage at the fellow's insolence.
"Until I know who you are I will speak to you how I like;" retorted weasel face.

The only thing that stopped Anthony giving the man a good whipping with his riding crop was the fact that all this time the gun had been pointing at his midriff! With difficulty he swallowed his pride realising that the situation was going nowhere and said stiffly; "If yer must know I am Sir Anthony Delusignan and I rode over specifically to see my old friend!"

"Well you've had a wasted journey then haven't you;" said weasel face, still with that impudent grin; "you had better be off before it gets dark," he indicated Anthony's horse with his gun.

Fuming impotently Anthony stalked stiff legged to his horse, untied it, mounted and clattered off back across the yard and out of the archway.

CHAPTER EIGHT

It was too late to ride home and he made his way to the Swan Inn at Stalham for a meal and a bed for the night.
The Landlord ushered him into the Snug and he was soon devouring a mutton chop, washing it down with a half decent claret.
After his meal he was shown up to his room; which though sparsely furnished contained a large comfortable bed!
He undressed and clambered gratefully into bed; it had been a tiring and trying day; however he could not get to sleep due to his anger because of the confrontation at the Grange and the shock of the demise of his old friend!
He determined to enquire of the landlord in the morning as to what had happened to poor old Turvey.
He lay listening to the church clock dolefully chiming out the quarters, halves and the hours till at last he fell into a troubled sleep.

He seemed to be in a small room, lit by a flickering fire; he was fighting for his life with a great brute of a fellow who stank of the grave; God, he was powerful and Anthony was tiring fast!
He managed to wrestle free and saw the man's face for the first time, or rather what was left of it; where the nose and eyes had been there was a large ragged hole!
Anthony opened his mouth to scream at this horror, but no sound issued from his mouth; then he was falling into a bottomless pit.
He was awakened by the landlord shaking him; "Thank God you are awake sir," he said concernedly, "we thought you wus a gonner, screamin' loud enough to wake the dead!"

Shamefacedly Anthony apologised; mumbling something about being under the doctor; he got dressed and went downstairs to pay his bill, adding a large tip to keep the fellow's mouth shut and left straight away, not stopping for breakfast.

   The weather broke just as he was crossing the bridge at Wroxham and he had to put on his waterproof.
The rain was breaking up the surface of the river and it looked as if it was in for the rest of the day.
It was a miserable journey home and he was cold and tired and very wet when he finally arrived.
He rubbed his old horse down, put a blanket on him and gave him a bowl of oats; then he let himself into the house which was in darkness.
Damn; he had quite forgotten that he had told Mrs.Neave he would be away for at least two days; lighting an oil lamp he got the stove going and boiled a kettle for some tea.
It was a filthy night with the rain lashing on the windows and the wind had got up and was wailing like a banshee; "not a night to be at sea," he mused; then he heard above the roaring of the wind that awful high pitched whistle!
He felt that a hand had clutched his heart and a picture of that ghastly face loomed into his mind; he now knew who the Watcher was.

CHAPTER NINE

Life at the Hall seemed to lift Anthony's spirits and when Magdalena told him she was pregnant he was overjoyed; this was what he had been waiting for; a son and heir to carry on the line!
They became inseparable; going everywhere together; so much so that his friends began to chide him for neglecting them; so a little conscious stricken he organized a Ball to show off his new bride.
For the next few weeks the arrangements went ahead; with much coming and going of visitors who wanted to see Magdalena and they were impressed by her lack of artifice and natural charm.
He took her to London to choose her gown for the forthcoming event and also to show her off to his Aunt Maude, she heartily approved; congratulating him on finding such a treasure!
So with the carriage laden with the results of her shopping expedition in Bond Street and a hefty cheque from his Aunt in his pocket they set off for the journey home.

On their return Magdalena immersed herself in preparations for the festivities and got him to help her with the invitations.
She was so excited at the thought of the forthcoming celebrations he worried that she might become overwrought and lose the baby; so he endeavoured to calm her down.
She would have none of it; "Antoni," she cried flinging her arms around him and kissing his nose;" let me be happy; do not worry about the little one, everything will be alright!"
The Ball was a glittering success and she stole the hearts of many of the young bucks.

He hardly got a chance to dance with her as she was constantly being whisked away onto the dance floor. He felt a pang of jealousy on more than one occasion at the attention she was receiving; but consoled himself with the thought that she would be tucked up in his bed when all the others had gone!
Finally the last dance had finished and everyone was complementing him on a wonderful evening and a beautiful wife.
They stood arm in arm at the door saying their goodbyes as the carriages departed down the drive. She suddenly shivered and he hurried to get her wrap; "come on my lass its getting cold and we don't want you getting a chill!"

   Magdalena was getting near her time and Doctor White drew Andrew aside one morning.
"I have no wish to cause you unnecessary alarm; but I am concerned about the position of the baby which may cause your wife difficulty during the birth!"
Alarmed Anthony exclaimed, "is there anything that can be done doctor, money is no object; get in anyone who can help you."
"Things should be alright providing I can turn the child prior to delivery;" replied the doctor, "you know I shall do everything in my power to ensure a safe birth!"
"I have every confidence in ye doctor;" said Anthony gripping his hand; let us pray that everything goes well."
Alas, things did not go well; Magdalena had a prolonged labour and despite the doctor's best efforts the baby was still born; the mother had lost too much blood and was sinking fast.
Anthony sat at her bedside holding her pale little hand; he was inconsolable; she whispered, "do not grieve for

me Antoni, you are still young and you will meet someone and love again."

"Never;" he cried "you are my only love;" he begged her to stay, but she lingered but a few hours and quietly slipped away; the baby had been a boy!

CHAPTER TEN

After the funeral he went abroad; he couldn't bear to be anywhere near the estate which had been the backdrop to this tragedy.
As he travelled through France and Spain his life consisted of doing anything which would blot out his memories of his beloved Magdalena.
He drank to excess; gambled and frequented houses of ill repute; never settling for long anywhere!
After one particular bout of drunken debauchery he awoke in a stinking alley and found that he had been robbed of all his money and the gold hunter which his father had given him had also gone!
Fortunately his letter of credit was lodged at his hotel; but this experience brought him to his senses.

He returned to the Hall to take up his responsibilities a changed man; no longer was he happy and carefree; but sullen and bitter with the world at large.
The servants avoided him whenever possible as he was irascible and uncommunicative when approached.
Not only that, but it was becoming evident that due to his extravagant life style the Estate accounts were rapidly going into the red!
It became obvious to him that he had to do something to reverse his fortunes after an acrimonious exchange with Craske, his Estate manager.
He was told in no uncertain manner want the position was; "if you don't find a solution within the next six months the estate will be in the hands of the Receiver!"
Armed with this unwelcome news he decided to do what many titled men did in similar straights; that was to marry a woman from the wealthy 'Trade Class' who were always on the look out for a Title!

He set off for the fashionable spa city of Bath where he hoped he would find his prey; attending many functions and taking the waters.
He was introduced to a certain Mr. Murgatroyd and his daughter one evening; apparently the man owned several iron foundries and loudly proclaimed his wealth at every opportunity!
His daughter Maria was plump; wearing hideous creations which did nothing for her looks and spoke with a broad Northern accent.
Anthony cringed at the thought of wedding this creature; but needs must when the Devil drives; so he applied himself to courting her and ingratiating himself with her father!
One morning they were taking coffee in the Pump Room when he felt a hand on his knee; on glancing down he saw it was Maria's!
God; he thought the baggage can't wait to get to it; all he felt was revulsion; it was the sort of obvious move a strumpet would make.
However it was too late to back out; his path had been marked out for him; so he pushed on with his courtship like a man facing the gallows!
In four weeks the banns had been read and they were married in Bath Cathedral.
His Father in Law got falling down drunk at the reception and had to be carried into a side room.
Anthony sincerely wished he could be in the same condition during the honeymoon!
As he wanted to return as soon as possible to the Estate they honeymooned in Weston Super-mare and what a week that turned out to be; the woman was insatiable, making every excuse she could to bed him!

CHAPTER ELEVEN

It was a very weary Anthony who arrived with his bride at the Hall; she on the other hand was full of life and energy; "I can't wait to see what our room is like;" she said.
He groaned inwardly at what was to come; "perhaps you can contain yourself long enough to meet the staff and have a meal?"
His irony was wasted on Maria who picked up her skirts and dashed up the steps into the main hall where she began to examine the furniture and paintings as if assessing their worth!
So began one of the worst periods of his life; she constantly chattered in that awful accent; embarrassing him in front of his friends with her coarse behaviour and being totally without inhibitions in bed!

He began to spend more and more time away from the Hall playing cards with his cronies and drinking in a vain effort to blot out the thought of what awaited him when he returned home.
Maria of course noticed and complained loudly about his neglect of her; particularly in front of the servants, which embarrassed him even more.
Things came to a head one night when on returning home he caught sight of one of the footmen leaving her room!
He confronted her and she just laughed in his face; totally unrepentant she said; "if you can't be a man I shall have to look elsewhere for comfort!
Stung by this reaction he responded; "you have a duty to me to uphold the honour and dignity
of the Delusignans."

"Honour of the Delusignans," she jeered; "if it weren't for my father's money you wouldn't 'ave a pot to piss in!"
She wagged her finger under his nose and hissed; "you had better mind your step wi' me my lad, otherwise I shall tell me father to cut you off wi'out a penny! Talkin' about money reminds me; I'm off to London for a few days to buy some new clothes so you'd better provide me wi' some cash!"
He stumbled out of the room speechless; realising that he was totally at the mercy of this unscrupulous harpy. He took his anger out on the footman by giving him a whipping and having him removed from his position in the household.

CHAPTER TWELVE

   Servant's gossip soon spread around the village that he was both a cuckold and a kept man and he became the butt of many cruel jibes.
He became a virtual recluse during daylight hours, only venturing out at night to call on a friend or acquaintance, constantly feeling ashamed and powerless to change the situation.
Maria made the most of her dominant position and took every opportunity to belittle or humiliate him; in turn he avoided her whenever possible and slowly his revulsion turned into a burning hatred!
As the summer days came she started to ride out alone to explore the countryside; "hope she falls off and breaks her fat neck; muttered Anthony glad that she was out of his way.

   He couldn't help wondering what had promoted her sudden interest in nature; it was totally out of character! So he decided to keep an eye on her movements, having noticed she nearly always rode through the woods at the rear of the hall and up the ridge beyond. Sure enough the following morning she had her chestnut mare tacked up and she set out; he quickly climbed to the uppermost turret at the back of the Hall and followed her progress through his spyglass!
He watched as she walked her horse up the ridge, threading between the sheep until she stopped outside the shepherd's hut.
The shepherd came out and lifted her down from the horse; he looked a powerful brute with a mop of shaggy black hair and craggy features.
He also seemed on very familiar terms with Maria and Anthony was left in no doubt why she was there; the

man's hands were all over her as he picked her up and carried her into the hut!

   This was the last straw; Anthony's rage condensed into a cold sustained fury; "she thinks she can snap her fingers at me does she; well we will see about that!" He ran downstairs and out to the stables; quickly tacking up his horse he checked the pair of cavalry pistols in the saddle holsters; mounted and rode out through the yard towards the woods.
On the way he calmly loaded and primed both weapons whilst he considered his course of action and the possible consequences; he would have to cover his tracks after the deed was done and have a story ready for Maria's sudden disappearance!
While he was thinking this out he emerged from the wood and made a wide detour that would bring him to the rear of the hut.
This would ensure that Maria's horse would not give the game away by whinnying; he slipped off his horse and silently stole up to the window and cautiously peered in.

   Sure enough they were entwined on a rough wooden bed oblivious to the world outside; he grinned to himself; "caught in the act by Jove!"
Standing in the doorway with hands on hips he remarked; "so this is what you call communing with Nature; I don't admire your taste, but then you never had any to begin with!"
The shepherd jumped to his feet, picking up a small shovel he advanced on Anthony with obvious malice in mind.
Anthony turned and ran round the side of the hut towards his horse; he heard Maria shouting; "beat him to a pulp the cowardly fool!"

The man was quick on his feet and began gaining on Anthony; but he reached his horse and pulled both pistols clear, cocking them he wheeled round and discharged both of them full in the face of his pursuer! The man dropped as if he had been pole axed, blood and pieces of bone covered the grass behind him.
Not stopping to look at his handy work Anthony strode towards the hut where Maria stood screaming hysterically outside the door.
He grabbed her by the throat and dragged her inside where he calmly began to strangle her; gradually all his anger drained out of him. As her lifeless body slipped to the floor he felt a great weariness come over him as he sat down on the rumpled bed.

CHAPTER THIRTEEN

He found some gunny sacking in the hut and wrapped it round the head of the dead man; then he cleared up the mess on the grass as best he could; animals and the weather would take care of the rest!
Next he carried Maria's body out to where the shepherd lay; he untied his horse and brought it over to the bodies.
He put them both on the nervous animal's back and led it to a small spinney on the top of the ridge.
There he dug a shallow grave with the shovel the shepherd had been carrying and then rolled both bodies unceremoniously into the hole, back filling and covering the soil with twigs and leaves until he was satisfied it was indistinguishable from the rest of the spinney.

There was one thing he had not considered in his plan and that was what to do with her horse; he couldn't ride back with it, on the other hand he couldn't turn it loose as it would simply make its way back to the Hall!
The solution suddenly dawned on him; if he took the horse over the ridge to the gypsy encampment he could sell 'em the horse and tack; they wouldn't ask questions, especially if they got it for a good price!
It worked like clockwork and he knew that with their natural reluctance to talk to 'Gorjas' they would keep his secret safe.
He rode a circular route back to the Hall as if he had been in the opposite direction to Maria; on arrival at the stables he asked the Groom; "has my wife returned yet?"
With a half concealed grin the Groom replied; "no sir, I expect she be still exercising!"

"Impudent fellow," thought Anthony; "he will be grinning on the other side of his face when the Estate is sold!"

He waited for a couple of days and then went to Fakenham to report that his wife was missing.
The Town Constable was an owlish looking man in his forties sporting a large military moustache.
He certainly had a well developed sense of his own importance and listened intently with what he fondly imagined to be a knowledgeable expression on his face. The result was that he looked more like an owl than ever and a stupid one at that!
He made copious notes whilst Anthony outlined the details; pausing with his pencil poised he asked; "may I make so bold sir; when did you actually last see your wife?"
"Damn the fellow;" thought Anthony; "I'm goin' to be here all day!"
"Two days ago," he replied, "she rode off on her horse in the mornin' and hasn't been seen since!"
"Perhaps she's stayin' with friends," suggested the Constable looking even more knowing as he scratched his nose with the pencil!
"She has no friends that I know of ;" retorted Anthony testily.
"What about family;" persisted the Constable warming to his task.
Delusignan exploded; "Look here just what are ye getting' at; are ye inferring that I have something to do with it?"
Realizing that he was exceeding his authority the Constable hastily assured Anthony that he was just trying to get to the facts of the case and intended no accusation!

"Right then; I am sure that we are both busy men so I will leave you to pursue your inquiries;" said Anthony rising to leave; " should you require further details kindly get in touch with Craske my Estate manager!"

"Craske," echoed the Constable licking the end of his pencil and laboriously writing it down.

As he came out of the building Anthony thought to himself; "with that blockhead in charge of the inquiry I have little to worry about!"

CHAPTER FOURTEEN

   He wrote to Maria's father asking if she had returned to the family home in Manchester and advising him of the situation.
Within five days Murgatroyd arrived at the Hall and immediately went for Anthony tooth and nail; accusing him of driving her out or worse!
Anthony waited calmly for his Father in Law to run out of steam before replying.
"In that case why should I have instituted the search by the local Constabulary in which I have taken part?"
"Also I have no wish to hurt your feelings; but it will soon become common knowledge that my shepherd went missing at the same time and the general opinion is that it was no coincidence!"
Murgatroyd blustered and threatened; but he knew his daughter's proclivities and had for the time being to accept the situation.
However he booked into the Feathers in the village so he could keep a check on the progress of the search!
The days dragged on without any further developments and it was generally assumed that the couple had dropped out of sight to avoid the repercussions that would surely follow discovery.
Murgatroyd had to return to Manchester for pressing business reasons; but not before he put a shot across his son in law's bows!
He arrived at the Hall in his carriage; strode into the morning room and thrust his bucolic face into Anthony's and hissed "Right you, no daughter, no brass and I still think you know more than you're sayin'.
With that he turned on his heel and swept out of Anthony's life for ever!

He called an emergency meeting with his Estate manager and told him what had happened.
"Then there is no possibility of the Estate being saved?" said Crask.
"Fraid' not unless my wife turns up, and that don't look likely," said Anthony, "in any case I'm not inclined to take her back in the circumstances!"
Craske nodded sympathetically and then asked; "what course of action does that leave you?"
"Only one;" responded Anthony; "and that is to sell the Estate; so if I were you I would start looking for alternative employment!"
Seeing the expression on Craske's face he added; "don't worry I will write you a glowing testimonial!"
The Estate was put into the hands of a London Firm of Auctioneers and a date was fixed for the sale in June. Anthony retained a small single story gatehouse for himself to live in and after the staff were dismissed he moved out of the Hall into his new home.

CHAPTER FIFTEEN

   Mrs.Neave shook her head as she prepared dinner for Captain Delusignan; he seemed to be getting even stranger of late!
He had taken to muttering to himself and starting up as if he heard something which she could not; his drinking had markedly increased and he always had that little green bottle handy!
Normally a scrupulously clean man he had neglected himself to the point where he had stopped shaving and began to smell!
He had also lost his hitherto hearty appetite and would absently pick at his food whilst continually listening for something or someone.
He was constantly preoccupied and she had difficulty gaining his attention.
In desperation one day she asked him what ailed him; he looked at her without seeing her and replied in a sort of monotone; "I am being pursued by the Hound of Hell!" with that he turned and went to the study window and looked out!

   The next day she determined to call in to see the doctor and inform him of the Captain's strange behaviour.
She was ushered into his surgery and he bade her sit down; "what can I do for you dear lady?" he enquired.
"I am very concerned for the Captain, I think he is losing his mind;" she replied and went on to describe the events of the previous day.
A frown crossed the doctor's face; "how long has this been going on Mrs Neave?"
"He has been odd since his second wife cleared off; but of late it has become much worse; could you go round and see him doctor?"

"I will call on him tomorrow after I have done my rounds; I must not miss poor old George Musset as he is failing fast and will soon be needing a priest's ministrations rather than mine I fancy!"
She left the surgery feeling somewhat comforted in the knowledge that she had done her Christian duty and could not be accused of neglecting the Captain!

CHAPTER SIXTEEN

When the doctor called Anthony the following day he was shocked by the man's appearance; Mrs. Neave had not exaggerated!
He was a travesty of the man he had known; gaunt, neglected in his personal appearance and absently picking up objects and fiddling with them.
"What is this?" said the doctor; "I never thought to see you brought to such a state!"
"I am a doomed man;" responded Anthony in an emotionless voice; " it is just a matter of time!"
"Come now this is not like the man I knew;" cried the doctor; "Bonaparte could not frighten you so why this loss of spirit?"

Anthony moved to the study window and beckoned the doctor with a badly trembling hand.
"Look ye down there doctor; d'ye see it down there at the bottom of the field by the gate?"
The doctor joined him at the window and looked out to where Anthony had indicated; "er I'm sorry, where did you say this thing was?"
Anthony turned, his face contorted with fear and his eyes blazing with terror; he gripped the doctor's arm in a vice like grip.
"There man, can ye not see it; down by the gate with a dog at it's feet?"
"What is it that you see?" asked the doctor.
"Why it is a dead thing with no face; why can't you see it?" as he spoke his voice rose to almost a scream!
He stumbled away from the window and the doctor sat him down in a chair before the fire and gave him a sedative.
He then went into the kitchen to have a word with Mrs.Neave; "is it possible for someone to sit with him

tonight as I fear that in his present state he may harm himself!"

She thought for a moment and replied; "I have to go and see to my husband's dinner, but I will call back to see that he is all right."

"Very well," said the doctor; "that will do for now; but if things get out of hand call me and I will come and see him, I fear that he has had some sort of brain storm which will require further investigation!"

"The sedative that I have given him should keep him quiet for now, but just in case I will leave you a second one to administer if required"

He bade her good evening and left for his home as the sun was beginning to set behind the wood throwing the trees into stark relief.

It was dark as Mrs.Neave set out for the Captain's cottage; there had been a shower and the trees along the way were dripping, making it wet under foot!

She shivered as she neared the place and something made the hair on the back of her neck rise; suddenly she heard the most appalling scream coming from the cottage; it sounded like some animal in it's death throes!

She almost fainted away at this terrible cry, but being a determined woman she began to run towards the back door.

It was wide open and at first all she could see by the flickering firelight was Anthony sitting bolt upright in his chair!

"Captain are you all right she called as she lit the lamp and brought it through from the kitchen.

Then she saw his face illuminated by the lamp; it was horrible, he had suffered a rictus which had frozen his face in an expression she would never forget!

His eyes bulged and his mouth was wide open still in the act of screaming; but that was not all; as she saw the muddy imprints of a man's bare feet and the paw marks of a dog coming across the floor to the chair, but none returning!

THE END

THE HAUNTED HUDSON

CHAPTER ONE

It was quite by chance that I came to acquire the rebuilt World War Two bomber; at the time it was the furthest thing from my mind!
I had been with my partner Sophie for two years and we decided to make the relationship legal and were in the throes of organizing the wedding; putting up the banns and the thousand and one details that go into tying the knot!
So when a friend of mine rang me one morning and offered me the opportunity of buying the plane I laughed in his face.
"You must be out of your mind Bob! You know Sophie and I are getting married; I can just imagine her reaction when I tell her that I have just bought another aircraft!
I already had a Harvard which I kept at North Weald at great expense; the insurance alone on those old crates is astronomic, as for the maintenance; ruinous!
However Bob persisted; "look old boy I wouldn't steer you wrong; this is the real thing, they dug it out of a bog in Norfolk and I have seen the restoration job they've done on it;
It is absolutely spot on; down to the Registration and Squadron numbers and price wise it's a snip!"
"In that case Bob why don't you buy it?"
He laughed and said; "I would old boy; but my doctor has put his oar in and I failed my last M.O.T. not allowed to fly without a qualified pilot with me!"
He continued; "I'm prepared to form a syndicate with you to buy and fly the damned thing; so you will only have to pay for half of it; what do you think?"

I must confess that I was tempted; a real Warbird; what a challenge and it was not as if I was paying the full price either!
"Where is this paragon at the moment?" I asked.
"Ah so you are interested," Bob crowed; "as a matter of fact it's hangared at a disused airfield near Catfield in Norfolk; we could wander down and have a shufti this week end if you like!"
Oh Bob you vile seducer; if I had known then what this decision was going to embroil me in I would have run away as far as possible from you!
"Fine;" I said and drove home full of excitement at the prospect of becoming the co owner of a twin engined Hudson!

My feelings of euphoria were somewhat dampened by Sophie's reaction when I told her; "you've done what!" she said in disbelief; "have you taken leave of your senses?"
She spent the next hour slamming cupboard doors in the kitchen as she prepared dinner and maintained an ominous silence for the rest of the evening!
When we got to bed I tried to lighten the atmosphere by saying; "I suppose a nibble is out of the question?"
She snorted and turned her back and switched off the bedside light; I suspected that this was a hint that the answer was no!

CHAPTER TWO

I picked Bob up next day and we set off up the M.11; it was a beautiful day and we made good time to Norwich.
We then became totally lost in the bye ways surrounding the coast North of Yarmouth and even the GPS appeared to have had a nervous breakdown as we finished up down a farm track!
Fortunately for us a local yokel on a tractor stopped and asked us; "are you a lookin' for anywhere in particlar' or just admirin' the view?"
Ignoring his rustic humour, I said; "as a matter of fact we are trying to find an old airfield in this area!"
"Ar, that u'd be Catfield; if yew look yonder there's a buildin' pairnted green; tha's where you want ter goo!"
Without a backward glance he was off; the tractor rounding a bend in the rutted track and disappearing out of sight!

We eventually found the entrance to the place and parked outside the hanger; which at first appeared to be deserted; but then one of the massive doors rolled back to reveal the Hudson in all it's refurbished glory!
A small man who looked in his fifties came out and walked towards us wiping his oily hands on a large cloth; clad in old khaki denims he looked the epitome of your average aircraft mechanic.
Bob strode forward hand extended to greet him; "hello Mr. Carswell this is my partner in crime Derek Penfold!"
Ignoring Bob's hand the man eyed me suspiciously and asked; "how many hours have you got on twins?"
Somewhat taken aback by the man's idea of social interaction I replied; er, none at the moment, but I intend to obtain them if and when I buy the plane."

"You'll need to; these old war birds ain't easy to handle; especially on take off or landing!"

"Oh; and I suppose you are an expert on this type are you?" I blurted out, stung by his attitude.

Carswell looked at me coolly and replied; "as a matter of fact I used to fly Hudsons when I was in the Fleet Air Arm; my log says that I completed four hundred and sixty hours on the type.

I stuttered my apologies as best I could and a fleeting smile crossed his face; "that's all right I'm older than I look; come on I'll show you round her; with that he turned and led us into the hangar.

The Lockheed Hudson was designed as a light bomber and used as a coastal patrol aircraft; the Fleet Air Arm used them for anti submarine duties.

She stood in the centre of the hangar resplendent in her camouflage and British roundels; there was that evocative smell of oil, rubber and dope associated with aircraft of that era.

Her two Wright Cyclone radial engines gleamed as if they had just been fitted at Lockheed's Burbank works in 1939!

I was in love; she was magnificent and I could hardly wait to fly her; but until I got the necessary certification she would remain unattainable!

Carswell opened the door in the side of the fuselage; pulled down an aluminium ladder and we all climbed aboard.

He moved forward and sat in the left hand pilot's seat, then beckoned me to join him.

I sat in the co-pilot's seat and he went through the control system with me; there seemed an awful lot of switches and dials to assimilate!

"Most of what you see had to be made or bought as there was not much of her that could be re-used due to being buried in the mud for so long;" he confided.
"Where did you manage to find all the parts?" I asked.
Mainly from Australia or New Zealand; he replied, they converted their Hudsons into transports after the War as they still had lots of spares, he replied.
I turned to speak to Bob, but he was not there; I was sure he had been standing behind me and I had a momentary shock!
Carswell looked at me and said; "are you all right, you look a bit peaky?"
"I'm fine;" I answered; "I was just wondering where Bob had got to; I could have sworn that he was behind me!"

CHAPTER THREE

Driving back Bob turned to me and said; "had a bit of a turn in the plane while we were looking round!
"What sort of a turn?" I asked.
"Well it sounds daft now; but when you were sitting up front I could have sworn that there was a guy in flying gear standing behind you; I felt a bit woozy so I went out for some fresh air!"
"Funny you should say that because I felt someone behind me and turned to speak, thinking it was you; but there was no one there;" I said.
"You don't think the plane is haunted do you?" said Bob slowly.
"I laughed; "don't be ridiculous Bob, whoever heard of a haunted plane!"
"No, it's a barmy idea;" he remarked, rather unconvincingly!
I dropped him off at his house still in a reflective mood; the incident had left him rather shaken it seemed.

When I got home Sophie was not there; she had left a note on the mantelpiece; "have gone over to mother's she isn't too well, will ring you later."
I had a look in the fridge and found a pizza two days over its use by date and bunged it in the microwave; obviously the 'Cold War' was still on!
Two days later after discussing it with Bob I rang Carswell on his mobile and told him we had decided to go ahead with the purchase of the Hudson.
"Can you fly her over to North Weald;" I asked him; I asked, we've organised hangar space for her there and we can finalise the deal over a spot of lunch!"
Carswell said he could; so it was arranged that he would bring her over the Thursday of that week.

Sophie came back on the Wednesday looking suitably smug now she had put me firmly in my place, things got back to what passed for normal; however when I mentioned that the plane was arriving the next day, she stalked into the kitchen and began shutting cupboard doors loudly; oh dear, here we go again!

We got down to the airfield at about nine thirty on the Thursday morning; the weather was not conducive to flying, with lowering cloud base and squally showers. Ten o clock came and went without the Hudson putting in an appearance and we began to worry!
I drove over to the Control Tower and spoke to the controller; "we have had no contact with her so far, but she may have been delayed by the weather;" he observed.
It was eleven forty when the Hudson finally descended through the clouds and joined the circuit; making a perfect three point landing!
"He certainly knows how to land a 'tail dragger' observed Bob admiringly as the plane taxied onto the apron outside the hangar.
Carswell cut the motors and the propellers gradually ceased to rotate; the door opened and Carswell jumped down and came over to us; "sorry I'm late;" he said, but I had a mag. drop on the port engine; anyhow I managed to fix it and here we are!

The aircraft was towed into the hangar and we went to look at our new toy; the rain water was trickling down the sides of the fuselage and off the wings, the engines were ticking as they cooled down.
I suddenly felt very proud to be the owner of this resurrected piece of history and couldn't wait to have a flight in her!

We all climbed into my car and sped off to a local hostelry for lunch and to settle the deal.

CHAPTER FOUR

Over lunch I asked Carswell if he knew anything of the history of the plane and how it came to crash.
"As a matter of fact I do;" he said, "when I bought it from the group of archaeologists who excavated it they provided me with a complete history of the Hudson and details of her final mission!
He went on to tell us that the aircraft had been seconded by S.O.E and diverted to a secret airfield in Norfolk in order to drop a couple of their operatives over Holland.
"Unfortunately shortly after take off she had engine failure and crashed into the marsh where she remained until the group found her and dug her up!"
"Presumably all onboard were killed?" I asked.
"Well, that's the odd thing;" he said, "everyone was accounted for except the pilot; his body was never found!"
"That's more than odd;" I said, "it's downright weird; how could he not be in the plane unless he baled out?"
"Well at the time it was thought he had perhaps been thrown clear, but despite several searches of the marsh his body never turned up!"
"It was 1944 and war time so I don't suppose we shall ever know what really happened;" he shrugged.

I made a mental note to contact the archaeologists to see if they could throw anymore light on this intriguing situation.
Carswell gave us all the paper work relating to the plane including the new Certificate of Airworthiness and we gave him the cheque.
We shook hands on the deal and Carswell promised to give me some tuition on the Hudson after I had passed the course!

We gave him a lift to Chelmsford where he caught a train back to Norwich.

   There was another note on the mantelpiece; when I got home; things were not looking too rosy apropos the wedding!
Most of the next month was taken up with my conversion onto twin engined aircraft and studying the Flight Manual which Carswell had thoughtfully provided.
I passed the practical and theoretical examinations; being checked out on a Beechcraft by a bored flight instructor who spent most of the flight yawning and trying to stay awake!
Things had been going badly between Sophie and me and the forthcoming marriage was beginning to look decidedly unlikely!
The last row we had ended in her shouting; "that ridiculous plane has become an obsession, I don't seem to be in the picture at all; well you had better make your choice, it's either the plane or me!"
Well it was no contest really; I couldn't bear to part with the Hudson now after all the trouble and money it had cost me, could I?"

CHAPTER FIVE

Carswell was as good as his word and at our request he travelled down to North Weald to give me my first lesson on the Hudson!
As I sat in the right hand seat whilst we waited at the end of the runway for clearance from the tower I felt a mixture of exhilaration and apprehension!
I turned to Bob and gave him the thumbs up sign as he sat in the bucket seat behind us and he gave me a somewhat sickly grin in return.
The headphones crackled as the tower gave us permission to take off and Carswll opened the Wright Cyclones up to full power!
The Hudson shook like a beast waiting to pounce on its prey; then he released the brakes and we began to gather speed down the runway.
The broken white line down the centre of the runway began to become a blur as she accelerated towards take off speed then the bumps suddenly stopped and we were airborne!
Carswell retracted the undercarriage as soon as we left the ground; "it cuts drag to a minimum in the climb out;" he said through the intercom.
Soon we were banking round the airfield gaining height; then he straightened out on a Northerly heading in a gentle climb; the outskirts of London and the great snake of the M25 out to our left.
We climbed to 5000 feet and he throttled back to cruising speed; "right Mr. Penfold she's all yours;" he said.
I put my hands onto the yoke and tried a gentle turn to starboard; the wing started to drop!
"Give her a little more power in the turn," said Carswell, these war birds are not as stable as civil craft!"

The flight lasted about an hour during which time we overflew Newmarket race course then we were heading back to the airfield.
I will land her Mr.Penfold;" Carswell said, "it's not easy doing a 'three pointer' on these; for one thing when you flare out you lose forward visibility due to the nose rising above the horizon!"

We came in over the boundary hedge and touched down without a bump; this guy really knew his stuff. We did two more flights that day as he talked me through the idiosyncrasies of this aircraft whilst I had control and gradually I became more confident; on the last flight even trying a slightly hairy landing!
Carswell did'nt seem perturbed and praised my progress, saying; "you really seem to have got the hang of it now; I think after a few more lessons I will have taught you all you need to know!"
I was really buoyed up by his comments and couldn't wait to go solo; my spirits were somewhat dampened however when I arrived home to find Sophie's suitcases in the hall!
She came down the stairs and gave me a withering look as she pulled on her gloves; "You have made your choice and so have I; obviously your old plane means more to you than I do; so I shall have to find someone who appreciates my for myself!"
I carried her cases out to the taxi; well it was the least I could do in the circumstances and stood while she sped away out of my life!

CHAPTER SIX

The following week I went solo; Carswell seemed to think that I was ready, patting me on the back as he left the aircraft his last words were; "don't forget to watch your speed in the turn; if in doubt give her more power!"
I called the tower for permission to take off and they confirmed; I trundled round the perimeter track and lined up at the end of the runway!
"Oil pressure 30 degrees, set boost and run up engines, check runway clear; full throttle; release brakes!
She leapt forward like a fat greyhound, gaining speed rapidly; the tail came up and shortly after she was airborne.
I pushed the retraction lever forward; checking the rotating wheels with a touch on the brakes and heard the reassuring thud as they went into their nacelles!
The climb was quicker with only one person aboard; I levelled out at three thousand feet and eased back the throttles to cruising speed.

The fields of Essex below me formed a patchwork quilt of differing shades of green and brown as they passed under my wings and above me the fleecy white cumulus clouds floated by.
This was the life; free as air and feeling like a God in my euphoric mood I sang at the top of my voice; then I remembered that I hadn't switched off the intercom!
I expect the staff in the control tower took a dim view of my noisy vocalisation, but they never mentioned it!
Just then, out of the corner of my eye I saw a movement in the cockpit; I quickly turned to my right

and saw for a split second, a grey outline in the co-pilot's seat; then it was gone!
"What on earth; am I going round the bend" surely Bob wasn't right when he asked the question about the plane being haunted?"
Shaken, I tried to pull myself together and concentrate on flying; I called the tower for permission to join the circuit and land; I began to lose height.
I managed to watch that my speed didn't bleed off in the turns and lowered the wheels on finals.

   The approach was good and I came over the boundary hedge and landed on main wheels only and waited for her to slow before pulling back the yoke to bring the tail wheel down.
I had to apply plenty of braking as the landing had been fast; then I realised that I had not lowered the flaps; whoops!
When I had taxied to the hangar and switched off I saw Carswell and Bob standing there and I didn't like the expression on Carswell's face; he looked annoyed!
"You do that again and you'll be through the fence on the other side of the airfield; what possessed you man to land without lowering the flaps?"
"I'm sorry, it was stupid of me, but I was distracted;" I said and then immediately regretted saying it!
"What do you mean?" he said.
"Er, I nearly had a bird strike;" "I lied; "a big fat seagull nearly flew into my port engine!"
"It was a good job you were on your own; if you had had a full crew aboard you simply wouldn't have been able to stop; he retorted, for heaven's sake keep your wits about you in future!"
When he had gone I told Bob the real reason for my actions; "I swear to you Bob that momentarily I saw a man sitting in the right hand seat!"

Bob looked worried; "what are we going to do old man, we can't have some spook flitting in and out of the cockpit willy nilly; it's off putting to say the least!" Apart from that I've booked a golfing holiday in Scotland next week and was going to ask you if we could fly up in this phantom ridden crate!"

CHAPTER SEVEN

As we flew over Manchester the grey clouds were scudding in off the Atlantic and it began to rain; it got worse as we crossed the Scottish border and the cloud base was down to one thousand feet.
"I shall have to climb and fly on instruments; there are some hefty hills in between;" I shouted to Bob.
We had decided to fly up in the Hudson after all; despite the advice from the Met Office; (they aren't always right)!
We climbed up through the clag into sunshine and I set a course for Edinburgh airport; so far we had not had any manifestations from the incumbent wraith!
We had booked into a B & B in Cumbernauld and intended to play a round or two at the local golf club.
I contacted the tower at Edinburgh and started to let down to join the circuit and was put into a stack as several commercial jets had priority.
  Eventually a cultured Scottish voice came over the intercom; "Hudson Delta Romeo; you are cleared to land; cross wind of four knots, thank you!"
I did remember to lower the flaps as well as the landing gear this time and we came in and touched down without incident!
She was the focus of considerable attention when we taxied onto the apron including several commercial pilots who plied us with questions about the old War Bird.
Eventually we managed to collect our golf clubs and extricate ourselves from the fans and went to collect our hire car!

  After a three day session of golf in which Bob only managed to break one club trying to get out of the rough, we headed back to the airport and took off to fly home.

I let Bob do the take off and we climbed to five thousand feet and levelled off; "this kite is a 'doddle' to fly," exclaimed Bob; "it's as if it's flying itself!"

I hadn't the heart to disillusion him; but on several occasions I had noticed the controls had been adjusted whilst he was checking other things!

In other words something was flying the plane apart from Bob; I checked to see if he had switched on the Automatic Pilot, but it was switched off!

"Watch your heading Bob;" I said, "you are beginning to change course to an Easterly direction.

"Good Lord; how did that happen; can't understand it;" he muttered bringing it back to its original course.

I could; it was obviously our mutual friend, the presence; it couldn't stop interfering; an implied criticism of our abilities no less!

I took control over Birmingham and flew the plane back to North Weald managing a decent landing with Bob still chuntering on about people not letting him complete the flight home as we touched down!

CHAPTER EIGHT

I didn't fly again for some weeks as the work had piled up and I had to clear the backlog.
By the time everything was back to normal and I could leave it in the capable hands of my secretary I was itching to take the Hudson up again.
I arrived early at the airfield that morning intending to visit a client in Rotterdam who was also a flying nut!
I filed my flight plan and walked over to the hangar and let myself in by the side door and crossed the floor to my plane.
The hair on the back of my neck rose; someone or something was testing the flight controls!
The ailerons; rudder and elevators were all flapping about; I couldn't see into the cockpit from where I stood; then common sense took over.
It was obviously a mechanic still working on the controls; yes that was it; I was panicking for no good reason!
I strode over to the door and opened it; "are you nearly finished?" I shouted; "I want to be away as soon as possible!"
Nothing; not a sound!
Apprehensively I climbed in and walked up the gangway into the cockpit; I instinctively knew there would be nobody there; I was right.
I slumped into the left hand seat; what was I going to do; fly with an invisible friend to Holland?
That way lay madness! I thought of Jimmy Stewart and his six foot rabbit; but that was acting; my aberration was real!
To take my mind off things I started to go through my pre flight checks before starting the engines; "I needn't check the flight surfaces as 'it' has already done that; I had difficulty suppressing a hysterical giggle!

Eventually I taxied out of the hangar; the doors having been left open for me; called up the tower and received permission to proceed to the end of the runway.
I ran up the engines, checked the oil pressure and manifolds; everything seemed fine.
The tower gave me the O.K.
And we were off; did I say we?
I climbed to cruising altitude and throttled back turning onto a heading that would take me to Holland.

  Passing over Harwich at eight thousand feet I continued to climb as the North Sea; looking cold and grey lay beneath me.
As I turned onto my new heading I looked towards the starboard wing; there, sitting in the right hand seat was a middle aged man in flying jacket, helmet and wearing a Mae West!
He had a thin face, a hooked nose and a neatly clipped military moustache.
He was looking straight at me with a sort of pitying expression; I must confess that I completely lost it; literally as the wing dropped and the plane dropped out of the sky as it went into a vicious spin!
The horizon was a blur, the cockpit was full of dust and debris whirling around and the instruments were unreadable all adding to my disorientation!
I panicked and froze on the controls; I had never been so frightened in my life; I looked at the spectre in despair.
He sat looking at me with that same expression for what seemed an age; then he leaned forward and took the controls from me stopped the rotation; he then opened the throttles and eased the nose down to regain flying speed.

By this time the sea was getting decidedly too close for comfort, but he eased back the yoke and she came out of the dive and we started to climb.
After regaining the cruising altitude he indicated that I should take back the controls; which I did rather gingerly, I was still shocked!
I checked my heading and then turned to thank him; but he had gone!

Bob and I decided that we had had enough excitement for one lifetime; so we advertised the Hudson on the Internet and it was eventually bought by an Australian sheep farmer from Wogga Wogga.
He came over to the U.K. complete with wide brimmed hat with corks round the rim and flew it back to his sheep station in Oz!
As we sat in the clubhouse I raised my glass and said; "here's to absent friends!"
"Amen," rejoined Bob, "Long may they stay absent!"

THE END

THE WHISPERING TREE

CHAPTER ONE

The village of Wiccan nestles in a picturesque valley some miles from North Walsham.
Surrounded by a large tract of ancient woodland' one could imagine that little had changed since the Saxons had settled there in the seventh century!
Life went on much as it had over the intervening years and many of the ancient customs and beliefs were still observed.
Christianity had come late to Wiccan, due to its remoteness and the stubborn following of the Saxon beliefs of tree worship and their ancient gods!
Successive priests had struggled manfully to change the attitudes of the inhabitants; but only gained a shallow tolerance of the religion.

   It was Lammas Eve and the young maidens of the village were in a state of suppressed excitement as this was the time they were about to visit the Whispering Tree to learn who they would marry!
The gnarled old oak stood alone in a large clearing in the wood; it was hollow and with its huge branches raised towards the sky it resembled a huge supplicant calling for Divine guidance.
The ritual had been going on ever since the village had been founded and was a tradition that was observed whenever girls reached puberty.
They would join hands round the tree wearing garlands of wild flowers around their brow and chant the ritual

words requesting the tree to divulge the information they yearned for!
Each girl in turn would approach the tree, bow three times, then put her arms around the tree and press her ear to the trunk.
Then if they were lucky (or imaginative) they would run from the tree calling to their friends; "I know; I know who my love will be!"
Others who were not so blessed wandered away from the tree with head hanging in deep disappointment.

   The ageing vicar turned a blind eye to this custom; having long since decided that he would make little mark on the attitudes of the locals.
The small Saxon church with its round tower and flint knapped walls stood on a slight mound just outside the village, where once had stood a Pagan temple.
The Reverend Hugh Williamson had come here as a Curate many years ago full of missionary zeal; but over the years, like a stone subjected to constantly flowing water he had eventually been worn into his present state of resigned acceptance!
He sighed as he laid out the hymnals for Sunday's Service; he knew that only the few old faithfuls would be occupying the pews again; "what's the point of it all?" he asked out loud, there was no response!

CHAPTER TWO

As she tripped happily towards the village from the ceremony Marion encountered old George Martin; he grinned exposing his few remaining teeth.
"Ha yer bin up ter the old tree then little mawther?" he asked.
She blushed and remained silent.
"I bet I can tell who yore goin' ter wed without the help o that there old tree; you ha bin mairkin sheeps eyes at boy Ralph since last Michaelmass;" he teased.
Seeing that she was embarrassed he touched her arm; "don't you tairk no notice o me little gal; I wuz just havin' a bit o fun tha's all; he's a good lad an I think he may have a bit of a sorft spot fer ye; mind how you go now!"
With that he shambled off towards the wood to check on his snares.
Marion reflected that the old man was sharper than he seemed; she did indeed have her sights set on Ralph!

The following Spring she was married to Ralph and they made a fine couple; he in his best clothes and her in her white dress and her hair garlanded with flowers. The whole village had turned out to celebrate the occasion and there was much feasting and dancing on the green.
Marion's father insisted on making a long rambling speech; frequently having to be reminded whom to mention, finally marring the occasion by raising his glass and keeling over backwards to the accompanying jeers and laughter of the company!
The young couple in the meantime had stolen away to be alone in the wood and reached the clearing where the old oak stood silhouetted in the moonlight.

For some reason Marion shuddered at the sight of the tree; the moonlight seemed to give it an air of menace! Ralph seemed not to notice having other matters on his mind; he drew her to him and as he was about to kiss her he noticed that she was looking intently at something over his shoulder.
"What is it my love;" he enquired; she made no answer so he turned to see what had frightened her.

   At first he could see nothing; but as his eyes became more accustomed to the gloom he was aware that something was emerging from the base of the tree! It seemed to grow before his eyes like a cloud of smoke; as he watched it began to assume human shape. He found he could neither move nor speak such was his terror; meanwhile the thing had formed into a living being and was moving towards them!
Ralph finally overcame his fear and shouted at the advancing figure; "what do you want of us?"
The figure made no reply, but continued to advance; Ralph could now make out that it was a man wearing a pair of tight fitting leather trousers; his upper torso was bare.
However this part of his body was covered in tattoos of birds, animals and Cabalistic signs, as was his face! On his head was a cap made of animal skin of some sort which came to a point on top of his skull!

   Ralph seized Marion's hand and prepared to flee; but she remained stock still watching the advancing figure. "For God's sake run Marion," he cried shaking her to break the spell; but she remained transfixed!
Throwing caution to the winds he flew at the figure intending to fight; there was a flash of light and he fell to the ground, his life blood gushing out of a severed throat onto the grass!

The figure continued to the girl and reached out to take her; as it did so she fell to the ground in a dead faint.

CHAPTER THREE

It was three days before the villagers became concerned as to the whereabouts of the newly weds and a search of the wood was begun.
It was noon when they came across the body of Ralph lying in the clearing where he had fallen.
Of Marion there was no trace and the search continued till the end of the week without success; eventually the village policeman was forced to call in the North Walsham force who in turn found no trace of her!
The atmosphere in the village became oppressive as neighbour eyed neighbour with suspicion, each wondering if the other was a murderer!
The Reverend Williamson endeavoured to restore an air of normality between the neighbours; but everyone was too engrossed in this terrible crime and its effect to listen!
People started to lock their doors at night and viewed everyone else with mistrust.
Rumours of strange happenings in the woods started to circulate and there were mutterings of a curse being put on the village.
"Tis the Pairnted Man I reckon; he's come back ter haunt us cos the people of the village put him ter death all them years ago;" said one worthy as they played cribbage in the Snug.
"Doant talk such a load of old squit Barney Medlar;" said the Landlady; "do you'll frighten people out o their wits!"
"As more likely to ha been someone who was a passin' through here that night who took Marion arter killin' poor Ralph;" said another; "arter all there's no one in the village who would ha done such a thing; is there?"

There was an awkward silence as they all began to think of possible suspects amongst them!

  It was in early November that one night old George Martin hammered on the door of the Red Lion just after midnight; the landlady opened her bedroom window and by the light of the moon saw the old man's face. It was contorted by fear; his eyes were starting out of his head and he was babbling incoherently whilst constantly pointing towards the wood.
She came downstairs and let him in; sat him down whilst she lit the lamp; she then poured him a stiff brandy and waited till he had drunk it.
She managed to calm him sufficiently to tell her what he had experienced.
He fiddled constantly with the tassels on the chair as he slowly told of the horrors he had seen that night.
  "I had gone up to check my traps about nine o clock an' warked my way through ter the clearin' where the old tree stand.
He paused for a few moments and then continued; "I had just tairken a couple o young rabbits and put em in my bag when I saw a pair o eyes a lookin' at me from that tree.
"Course; I thought that were a stag as there are plenty of em about at this time o the year' but I still felt a bit afraid like!"
"Then this thing come out of the shadders an' I could see it weren't no stag, that were a man!"
He paused and put his head in his hands, then slowly raising his head he looked the landlady full in the face and said; "I swear by all that I hold dear that this man was like no other I ha' ever seen!"
"He were nairked apart from his trousers and he were covered in pictures all over his body and his fairce; I just let out a holler and ran for me life!"

The landlady involuntarily put her hand to her face; "My God George yew ha' seen the Pairnted Man; and to think that I told old Barney Medlar that he was talkin' squit the other night when he mentioned it!"
She made up a bed on the settle downstairs for him and the next morning he was sufficiently recovered to go home.
The story soon got around the village and the peoples fear was palpable; to make matters worse another girl went missing!
Little Amy Fuller had gone to her grandma's cottage to take her some home made preserves just as the sun started to set.
When she did not return her father set out to find her; but the only thing he found was her basket lying by the path, the contents scattered on the ground.
He raised the alarm and the men of the village set out with torches to find her; but of little Amy there was no sign!!

CHAPTER FOUR

The Parish councillor called a village meeting to decide what action to take; feelings were running high and accusations were flying back and forth!
He managed to calm them down somewhat by shouting over the hubbub; "nawthin 'll git done if ye all shout at once; do you calm down and ye'll have a chance ter speak one at a time!"
There were all kinds of wild suggestions made; but no one seemed to have anything constructive to say.
The meeting finally broke up without any clear idea of what to do.
 Albert Gittins the local policeman was told in no uncertain terms what the villagers thought of the police force and feared for his personal safety after someone threw a brick through his window whilst he was having his tea!

The Reverend Williamson on the other hand had thought long and hard about the matter and decided to fight fire with fire!
He had searched through his extensive collection of books and found a treatise on ancient religions, where he discovered valuable information regarding Wicca or Saxon magic!
Later that evening as dusk was falling he left the house wearing his cloak over his chasuble.
He had a silver cross; a Bible, a phial of Holy Water and a candle all in a Gladstone bag as he strode purposefully towards the wood.
 The wind was increasing to gale force and dark clouds were scudding across the sky with the occasional flash of lightning in the distance.
He was alone and afraid, but he was sure that his Faith would prevail and pressed on through the worsening

weather towards the clearing where the ancient oak was waving its branches wildly in the increasingly strong winds!

He stopped several yards from the tree; raised the cross and started to recite the words of the ceremony of Exorcism!

By now the wind was roaring through the wood like a wounded animal accompanied by vivid flashes of forked lightning which illuminated the old man; his white hair and cloak flying in the gale and his upturned face wet with the first drops of the oncoming rain! Undeterred he continued to speak whilst at the base of the tree something was beginning to materialise!!

The priest trembled as he saw the figure taking shape before him; but he continued.

The Painted Man advanced towards him and as the priest looked into those terrible red eyes he suddenly felt his strength and resolve draining from him; with a great effort of will he averted his gaze whilst continuing the ritual.

The strength of his adversary was overwhelming; he could literally feel the waves of evil being directed at him constantly!

The creature was almost on him and was reaching out its arms to grasp him when the old man removed the stopper from the phial of Holy Water and flung its contents into the face of this foul fiend!

Simultaneously a mighty bolt of lightning struck the oak splitting it down the middle and setting it alight!

The Painted Man screams were so loud that the Reverend Williamson fainted away and it disappeared in a cloud of black smoke.

The Priest slumped to the ground utterly drained and lay motionless as the storm raged around him!

CHAPTER FIVE

He was found in the clearing next morning by Constable Gittins whilst on his rounds; he raised the alarm and the Reverend was respectfully carried back to the Rectory.
A doctor was called as the old priest had not regained consciousness, but he was alive, though his breathing was shallow!
It was two days before he came round and could tell the villagers what had happened on that fateful night

When they examined what was left of the tree amongst the ashes they found the remains of a burial; the body had been buried facing downwards and they found bits of iron scattered around it; indicating that whoever it was had been a witch or warlock of some kind!
A knowledgeable villager remarked; "they do say that in the olden days people believed that iron was protection against Black Magic!"
Everyone nodded sagely as they gathered up the bones and burned them on a funeral pyre; they were also aware that fire cleansed evil!
The sequel to this event was also most strange as a few days later the two missing girls showed up; but neither could remember where they had been or what had happened to them!
Marion eventually remarried and had several children; however the local midwife noticed that they all carried a strange birthmark that looked remarkably like a tattoo!

THE END

REMEMBER ME

CHAPTER ONE

The Ballantyne Theatre; named after its founder Ambrose Ballantyne, the illustrious Shakespearean actor was an institution of enlightenment and culture. Situated in an ancient alley in the heart of Norwich City; boasting an Elizabethan exterior, an apron stage and a minstrel's gallery, it had been performing plays of a high standard to lovers of the theatre for almost two centuries!
Although well patronised the rise of running costs and the decline of ageing audiences was a continuous concern to the constant procession of theatre managers!
"Takings were down again this week dear;" so said Millicent Ogilvy as she swept into the manager's inner sanctum.
She was a lady of indeterminate age; but the skilful application of makeup and the marvels of her corsetry belied her advancing years!
Gilbert Wyndham looked up wearily, unconsciously brushing his lock of unruly hair from over his eyes; he presented an aesthetic figure with a long suffering artistic face; he sighed, " when are you going to bring me some good news Millie, I've just had the bills in for the repairs to the roof and the rewiring in the auditorium!"
Millicent made sympathetic noises as she dumped the cash box on his desk; "trouble is dear the youngsters are simply not interested in the theatre these days!"
She turned to leave and then paused; turning she said resignedly; "by the way dear Lawrence fluffed his lines again last night, people are beginning to complain!"

Gilbert groaned; "Oh God! As if I haven't enough problems already; you know the trouble Millie, he's been here for donkeys years; part of the fixtures and fittings in fact; how on earth do you fire an institution?"

"The fact of the matter is that he should be in an Institution;" answered Millicent tartly; "he is just too old and going senile to boot!"

"I'll have a word with him," Gilbert replied absently; Millicent sniffed disbelievingly and swept out!

It was always a difficult and embarrassing task persuading old actors to leave the profession when they had passed their 'sell by date'!

Apart from hurting their pride, often they had no funds put by for their retirement and were condemned to live in genteel poverty wherever they could find a berth. Gilbert was loath to broach the subject as had been several managers before him!

CHAPTER TWO

Lawrence Gillespie sat near the window of his room trying to thread a needle; screwing his eyes up in order to insert the wool through the eye of a needle for the umpteenth time.
"Drat the pestilential thing," he exploded; he had already lost count of the number of attempts he had made.
His sock lay across his bony knee displaying a large hole in the toe; a silent advertisement to his failure! With a final expletive he threw the needle down and put his sock back on; time was getting away and he would soon have to go to the theatre.

He was appearing in a modern production of Hamlet as the Ghost and he liked to get there early so he could run through his lines!
He had stumbled over them in last night's performance and the director had admonished him.
"After all you couldn't have a part with less to say, unless you were a spear carrier!" he had said.
"What an insult to a man of my experience;" he thought bitterly as he donned his coat and hat.
As he came down the stairs his landlady emerged from her den; she was a blowsy, common sort of creature and she reeked of cigarette smoke.
"I'm glad I caught you Mr.Gillespie, there are two weeks rent owing on yer room; "I shall expect it payin' on Friday at the latest otherwise I shall have to consider my position and yours!"
Leaving her still ranting in the hallway he hurried out into the street; "what an old harridan," he thought, "why am I subjected to such harassment; a man of my calibre being insulted by such an old slattern."

Truth was that type of confrontation had been all too common during his acting career due to the financial uncertainty of his profession!

He walked to the theatre arriving in the Green Room to find no one had yet arrived.
Good! He would go up to the dressing room and change into his costume, do his make up and then study his lines.
As he climbed the stairs he felt a sudden pain in his chest which seemed to spread down his left arm; reaching the top he slumped down in a chair in front of the long mirror and looked at his reflection.
He was shocked; the face that looked back at him was chalky and drawn and there were dark rings under his eyes; the pain struck him again making him sweat!
Picking up his make up bag he scrabbled desperately for the packet of aspirin he kept there.
Lawrence took the tablets into the toilets to get some water; but as he reached the sink the pain hit him suddenly and he dropped the tablets and clutched his chest.
The pain was now unbearable so he went into one of the closets and sat down and shut the door, he didn't wish to be seen like this; he knew only too well how tongues would wag amongst actors and he couldn't afford to lose his place in the theatre now!

Just in time; as the sound of voices and footsteps hailed the arrival of two of the principal players.
"I thought I saw old Gillespie creeping up the stairs as I came in;" said one.
The other person laughed; "probably come to learn his lines after getting a wigging from Gerald last night!"

"I'm not surprised; he gets worse, he's lost his timing as well; everyone starts to sweat when it's his turn to speak; the delay is almost palpable!"
Lawrence was dimly aware of the conversation as he slipped into unconsciousness while his tired old heart tried to keep his blood circulating.

CHAPTER THREE

He was back home in Salisbury as a young man listening to a tirade from his father about his decision to become an actor.

"The acting profession so called, is made up of rogues, vagabonds and harlots; if you are seriously considering going ahead with this madness I shall disown you and cut you off without a penny!"

"I paid for your education at Saint Jude's and expected you to follow my example by entering the Church to a life of selfless devotion to others, as I have done!"

"Father I have no desire to become a clergyman; this is the profession I wish to follow and have already been offered a place with a travelling Repertory company!"

His father would have none of it, and being a clergyman of the 'Fire and Brimstone' brigade he turned Lawrence out of the house despite the weeping protestations of his wife and daughter.

He joined the group and began touring the country learning as he went along; after a couple of weeks the Actor Manager decided that he was safe to speak a few lines in a Restoration play.

He managed to say his lines and went on and came off without colliding with the props or his fellow actors! Soon he was given greater responsibility, such as playing minor characters in Shakespeare and the like; within a year he was regarded as a flourishing actor. He loved the life despite the hardships of constantly being on the move; often being hungry and short of money; but like Mr. Micawber before him he was content to wait until something turned up!

He wrote letters to his mother and sister when he could and collected the replies at the next town he was playing.

The years flashed by and he felt happy and fulfilled; then one night when they were playing Much Ado in Bolton he was approached by a Theatrical Agent!
'Solly' Goldstein was typical of his ilk, wearing a loud tweed suit with a mustard coloured waistcoat; across his ample girth stretched the chain of an expensive gold hunter which resided in his left waistcoat pocket.
Smoking a fat cigar he walked up to Lawrence and extended a pudgy hand bedecked with large rings.
"My boy;" he boomed, "I pride myself on recognising talent when I see it and you got it!"
Ushering the overwhelmed young man to a table and ordered drinks; fishing a card from his pocket he passed it over.
Prodding the card with a stubby finger he said rather unnecessarily
; "that's me that is, twenty years in the business; know everybody who is anybody and I can make you a star in no time at all if you sign up with me!"

Lawrence was at a loss; having fame and fortune waved under his nose was a new experience and he had mixed feelings about it.
On the one hand he was flattered; on the other his innate loyalty to the group tugged at him, he liked the camaraderie and the feeling of belonging to something!
He stammered, "thank you Mr. Goldstein for your confidence in me; but I assume it would mean leaving my present position and I owe the company a great deal.
"Your loyalty does you credit my boy;" boomed Goldstein; "but with your presence on stage you tower above the rest!"
"You owe it to yourself to grasp this opportunity I'm offering you, it may not come again!"

"Can I sleep on it and ring you in the morning; it's all a bit overwhelming at the moment and I would like to think it over!"

"If you must my boy; but don't take too long about it as I am a busy man and have others to see;" he stood up and shook Lawrence's hand; "you have only to pick up that phone tomorrow and your future will be assured!" He waved his hand as he departed leaving Lawrence in a whirl of questioning and self doubt.

CHAPTER FOUR

He didn't sleep much that night and next morning he talked it over with Mr.Travis the Manager.
"Well my boy it's not for me to say; you are the one who has to make the decision; it's a big step, whereas your employment here is assured for the foreseeable future!"
"Apart from that we would all miss you as you have fitted into our little troupe very well and are beginning to repay some of the time and money we have invested in you!
Lawrence felt guilty, he couldn't let them down after all that Mr. Travis had said; he stood up and said that he had thought it over and would inform the Agent of his decision!
Travis heaved a sigh of relief as Lawrence left; truth was that the takings had been going up well in recent weeks and the boy had no idea of his worth!

"I think you must be barmy turning down an offer like that;" said Connie Manning as she buffed her nails. "You have the talent to go far Lawrence and I'm not just saying that; I suppose old Travis talked you out of it!
Smarting somewhat from her remark he retorted; "No he did not, I like being part of this troop, it's the first time in my life that I have felt that I belonged somewhere!"
"Well, I just hope you don't live to regret it that's all; acting is a very precarious profession and Fame and Fortune come very seldom;" she said turning her attention to her nails once more.

The years rolled by and Lawrence settled into the routine of the touring actor; he didn't go home any

more now as the last time he had called his father slammed the door in his face!
His sister came running down the road after him and they clung together while the tears fell.
"How is Mother?"
Cecily replied between sobs; "she is not well Lawrence; I think it broke her heart when father…."
"I know, I know;" he said, "please tell her that I love her and think of both of you often; I'll write as soon as I get to the next venue; God bless you both!"
His heart was heavy as he travelled back to Birmingham; where they were putting on two plays per day with a change mid week!

Things were also about to change very soon in Europe; it was 1939 and War Clouds were gathering over Europe and the Germans were on the rise again! Chamberlain had returned from Berchestgarten waiving his little piece of paper "Peace in our time" and Britain heaved a sigh of relief.
However it was to be short lived as the Nazis rolled into Czechoslovakia and the rest of the world woke up to the fact that it would not end there!
All over Britain feverish preparations were being made to protect public buildings and create shelters for the populace.
As far as Lawrence could see the Theatre became more popular, as if people were using it as a means of blotting out the horrors to come!
Finally on the 3rd of September Hitler invaded Poland despite being warned of the consequences and Britain was once more at war.

CHAPTER FIVE

   Lawrence was on the horns of a dilemma; on the one hand he wanted to do his bit for his country; but another part of him didn't want to leave his adopted family, the Rep!
However after the 'Phony War' ended and the fighting in France was at it's height he couldn't stand by any more.
He went to the local recruiting office and enlisted in the army; the troop laid on a farewell party at the Dog and Duck and he received a warm hug and kisses from all the girls!
He caught a train for the Army barracks at Catterick where he was kitted out and did eight weeks training before embarking for France.
Disembarking at Dunkirk his Battalion were immediately sent to prevent the Germans crossing the river Meuse.

   The German tanks came through the Ardennes bypassing the Maginot Line leaving the French sitting in their concrete bunkers with egg on their faces!

The Germans overran the French and British lines and Lawrence found himself in what was left of the British Expeditionary Force making his way to the coast!
After many near squeaks he arrived on the beach at Dunkirk again; he was shocked by what he saw.
There were literally thousands of men amongst the dunes waiting for something to happen, constantly being bombed and strafed by the Luftwaffe; it was chaos and no one seemed to be in overall charge!
 Day after day hundreds of men stood in the sea awaiting rescue whilst Stuka dive bombers constantly

bombed them; it was like a picture from Danté's inferno.
Then the miracle happened; every ship and boat that could be mustered started to come across to pick up our army from the beaches, it was a triumph of improvisation!
Despite the terrible losses of ships and men at the end of it they had rescued over 300,000 soldiers off the beach it was nothing short of a miracle!
Lawrence was pulled aboard a cabin cruiser owned by a retired naval officer after standing in the water for hours, despite being strafed by a German fighter they returned safely to Portsmouth.

He was returned to his unit and after a period of retraining they were kitted out with desert gear and shipped off to Egypt to fight Rommel!
He survived the battle of El Alamain and next found himself fighting in Italy where he was injured by a mortar round which exploded nearby.
After recovering in a military hospital he was found to be unfit for combat duties; but then had a stroke of luck!
The Medical Officer was organising a Concert Party for the wounded and asked for anyone with stage experience.
Lawrence offered his services and was later transferred to ENSA (military Entertainment).
He appeared in Reviews, short plays, monologues; he even sang in concert parties and this experience helped his full recovery.

When the war finally ended he was discharged and found himself standing in Leicester Square in his demob suit with a five pound note in his pocket and nowhere to go!

He did the rounds of the agencies; but the entertainment business had changed and was still recovering from the restrictions of wartime.
Like many of his compatriots he applied for work at the Windmill; but they preferred comedians or novelty acts to legitimate theatre actors.
He managed to get himself an agent who provided him with bits of work; but it was a struggle to earn enough to keep the wolf from the door!
Then he saw an advert in the Stage requesting experienced actors ready to commence with a theatre in Norwich.
With just enough for the fare he turned up at the Ballantyne for interview and was given a one year contract subject to review!

CHAPTER SIX

He found himself 'diggings' with a widow on the outskirts of Norwich and settled into a pleasant routine; he found Norwich very amenable and enjoyed socialising with other members of the company.
The contract was renewed and extended for five years and he became one of the pillars of the Theatre; appearing in most of the productions!
Thus his life settled into a pleasant routine; but as we all know things can change suddenly, and indeed fate intervened when his landlady was taken seriously ill!
She was diagnosed with cancer and lingered for a few months before passing away.
Lawrence was devastated having been genuinely fond of her; to cap it all at the funeral her son informed him that the house was to be sold and that he would have to seek lodgings elsewhere!
He managed to find himself a room in one of the shabbier parts of the city, but it was nearer to the Theatre so he could save on bus fares.

So the years rolled by and he settled into a sedentary sort of existence; he would often drop into the little Bistro within the Theatre for a light meal and a chat with fellow actors and the staff behind the bar.
People who knew him always said that there was something sad about him; as if he were nursing a personal tragedy of some sort.
Not that he was unsociable; far from it, he always had a kind word for everyone and a sympathetic ear for those that sought it!
His father and mother had passed away years ago and his sister had married and moved to Australia on the £10 Government Scheme shortly after the war.

They still kept in touch by letter; but it was not the same and he longed to see her again; she did in fact urge him to come out and see her and her husband; but he could not afford the fare or spare the time from the theatre.

  Then in his latter years his memory began to fail him; he found playing very wordy parts challenging and actually had 'dries' during Shakespearian productions; it is an excellent actor that can ad lib his way out of that!
The word got around that Lawrence was 'unreliable' and successive managers began giving him smaller and smaller parts.
No one however considered getting rid of him because of his long service to the Company; so there it was; an impossible situation!

CHAPTER SEVEN

The cast were beginning to panic no one could find Lawrence; his costume was still hanging on the rail in the changing room. It was decided to get one of the younger players to cover for the ghost of Hamlet's father and the Prompt to read his lines.
"I'll swing for that old fool if I get my hands on him," said the director; "he's probably taken the huff after I told him off last night and not bothered to turn up!"
"No, he is in the building, at least he was when I arrived;" said Simon Craig who was playing Polonius; "I saw him coming up the stairs!"
The Final Call came and the actors trooped downstairs to get into position backstage; "It's a full house tonight dears;" said Millicent standing at the bottom of the stairs; "Break a leg!"

The house lights dimmed and the curtain rose on Act One, Scene One, "Elsinore a platform before the castle; the play began.
During Scene three the Director called to the young understudy; "Tony you had better get into the wings ready for your entrance; the prompt will read the lines!"
A few minutes later Tony returned looking puzzled; "Lawrence is already there Gerald, standing in the wings!"
"Thank God," Gerald mopped his brow; "I shall have words with him when he comes off; does the Prompt know?"
"Yes he saw him too;" Tony responded; "right I'm off to get this clobber off it weighs a ton!"

Scene Four arrived and Hamlet, Horatio and Marcellus awaited the appearance of the ghost, finally

coming to the line; "Doth all the noble substance off and out to his own scandal,"
Right on cue Lawrence appeared stage left, he seemed to have done a wonderful job with the makeup; he was ghastly white; his eyes seemed glazed over and his face was drawn with pain!
Horatio was momentarily shocked and nearly missed his cue; he pulled himself together and spoke the line; "Look my Lord it comes!"
The rest of the scene passed off without further incident.
Then onto Scene Five; Hamlet's conversation with the ghost; Simon marvelled at the strength of Lawrence's voice, his responses being delivered in such sepulchral tones that they sent shivers down the backs of the audience!
His final words being; "Remember me;" his performance brought the house down and the audience gave him a rousing ovation as the scene ended.
The performance was a triumph; and the cast took five curtain calls at the end; Gerald was cock a hoop!
   "That cunning old fox has been hiding his light under a bushel; that was the greatest performance of all time; including Larry's film version!"
"Go and flush him out where ever he is and bring him down to the bar; he deserves a drink, in fact several!"
Rubbing his hands together Gerald went out of the Green Room to mingle and bask in the reflected glory of Lawrence's performance.
It was Tony who discovered Lawrence's body in the cubicle; he had obviously been dead for some hours as Rigor Mortis had set in!
He ran down the stairs shouting the news and went to ring for an ambulance.

THE END

DARK LANE

CHAPTER ONE

My name is David Goodwin; I work in the City of London and live alone in Shorditch.
My wife and I went our separate ways two years ago and I have become used to the solitary life of a bachelor.
Friends say that I am somewhat of a recluse and maybe they are right as I sometimes avoid company depending on what mood I am in.
A morbid change seemed to come upon me during the Great War; I saw horrors that a sane man should not see during the battle of the Somme and was invalided out suffering from shell shock.
The doctor said that with care I should return to a normal way of life; but somehow that seems to have eluded me.
My landlady is a cheery soul and keeps me on an even keel with her constant chatter and motherly care.

One morning before Christmas she bustled in with my breakfast tray, as she set it down I noticed a letter next to the marmalade.
"Here you are Mr. Goodwin, somebody is thinking of you," she said handing it to me.
On opening the lavender coloured envelope I was aware of a whiff of perfume; it was a delicate aroma, not one of those scents that overpower the senses!
I took out the letter and unfolded it, noticing the spidery writing, obviously that of an elderly female.
Sure enough it was from my Aunt Felicity who lived in some obscure place in Norfolk!

What on earth did she want? I had not heard from her since my wife had left me and had assumed she had passed over.
Far from it; she was inviting me to spend Christmas with her and Mr.Moggs (a large black cat)!
She doted on this animal and chattered away to it all day; in times gone by she would have been branded a witch and Mr.Moggs her familiar!
"I am sure the change of scenery will do you good and the fresh air will chase away that London fog; company for us both; good to see you again etc.
The letter rambled on interminably; so I skipped to the last paragraph which gave instructions about train times and changes.
Good God she must have scoured Bradshaws to get such detail!
She finished the letter with a strong plea not to decline the invitation as this might be the last time that we will have to meet in this life; was she terminally ill?
Why had I begun to wonder if I was in her will? I pushed the thought deep into the recesses of my mind!

   My first reaction had been to send her a brief note declining her request; but then the thought of spending the Festive Season alone again loomed large!
Every Christmas Mrs. Banks closes her house and goes to stay with her brother Charlie in Penge.
That meant that I had to stay at the Club amongst a load of old bores constantly reminiscing about the 'Old Days,' yeagh!
So finishing breakfast I went to my room and composed a letter of acceptance to Aunt Felicity, put on my hat and coat and went out into the cheerless morning to post it.

CHAPTER TWO

As the train pulled out of Liverpool Street station and began to gather speed, passing the interminable backs of sooty terrace houses the leaden skies seemed to reflect the general air of hopelessness hanging over the scene.
It had started to snow and the flakes that settled on the carriage windows began to melt and streak across the glass like Angel's tears!
I shivered and drew my overcoat around me; it was chilly here in the carriage and I assumed the train's heating system was not working properly.
My only companion was a clerical gentleman sitting opposite me; beside him was a small suitcase which I offered to place in the rack; he gratefully declined keeping one hand firmly on the lid!
We chatted in a desultory manner during the journey, but when I spoke of going to Norfolk his ears pricked up.
"Why that is most interesting," he said leaning forward and looking earnestly into my eyes; "might one enquire where that might be?"
I told him and he waxed quite lyrical saying; "I know the area well having served as curate to the incumbent Rector at Aylsham; a beautiful church with many fascinating connections!"
When I mentioned the name of my Aunt's village his expression changed; it was as if a cloud had passed across his face.
He seemed loath to discuss the matter further and the conversation lapsed into an uneasy silence.

As we drew into Ipswich station he stood up and picking up his small case he turned and said; "be on your guard whilst you stay with your relative, Norfolk

is a mysterious county which still holds onto many strange superstitions and beliefs!"
Before I could ask what he meant he had slipped into the corridor and was gone.
Somewhat mystified by these warning words I determined to quiz Aunt Felicity on arrival!
My carriage began to fill up with local people whose strange dialect confounded me; I closed my eyes and was soon asleep.
I must have slept soundly because the next thing I was aware of was being shaken roughly by the arm; "weark up sir this is Narwich; I teark it you doant wish ter goo back ter Lunnon?"
"Er.No;" I replied looking in to the face of the ticket collector; he asked me where I was headed and advised me that the next train to Aylsham was due in forty minutes!

    Having checked which platform my train was departing from I made my way to the Buffet and ordered a cup of tea.
Looking out of the window I saw that the snow was still falling; although it was now beginning to lay and it was also growing dark; I sincerely hoped there would be some sort of transport at the end of my journey!
Eventually the local train puffed into the station and disgorged its passengers, all hurrying to get home out of the weather.
I picked up my case and walked down the platform to board the carriage next to the engine; there seemed to be no other passengers entering the train which seemed odd!
A few minutes later the guard blew his whistle and the train jerked forward and began to pull out of the station.

We were travelling alongside the river which looked cold and hostile; by now there was a covering of snow on the countryside and the sky looked full of menace! The train crossed the river and the line seemed to swing away and began to take us in a Northerly direction.
The wind was increasing and playfully blew the smoke from the engine in all directions as we journeyed through cuttings and under bridges; in places the trees overhung the track, sometimes brushing the tops of the carriages!
We occasionally stopped at some wayside station or halt; but no one either got out or got in whilst the snow continued to fall silently on the bare countryside.
A feeling of unease was beginning to permeate my mind; as if someone or something was waiting to do me harm!
   I tried to brush this feverish fancy from my brain, telling myself that it had no basis in fact!
I was still wrestling with my equilibrium as the train drew into a large station and I caught sight of the title **AYLSHAM** on the passing hoardings.
On alighting I looked around for a porter or someone who could advise me where to obtain transport!

CHAPTER THREE

By now the wind was roaring around blowing the snow in all directions as I made my way down the platform to the exit.
As I came out of the station I saw a horse drawn cab standing under the gas light; the horse looked half starved and hung its head against the driving snow.
My eyes were drawn to the driver who sat motionless on his box, his face obscured by the turned up collar of a large frock coat.
He sat with his whip clutched in his bony hand looking neither right nor left; it could have been a painting such was the immobility of the scene!
However I was getting covered in snow and it had become bitterly cold, so I strode up to the cab and climbed in.
I shouted directions to my Aunt's cottage and at first the driver made no movement; thinking that the wind had carried my words away I shouted as loudly as I could!
This seemingly had the desired effect and he whipped up the horse and we moved off into the worsening weather.

By now drifts were beginning to form along the narrow country road, spilling off the surrounding fields causing the driver to take evasive action to avoid getting stuck.
We travelled in this manner for what seemed an age until he came to a sudden stop.
On looking out I perceived that a large drift was blocking our way; on shouting to him what he intended, he indicated that he would go no further!

I asked how far my Aunt's cottage was and he pointed to a lane running off to the left which still seemed passable.

I started to get back into the cab, but he shook his head and waved me away; what sort of man was he to abandon his passenger in this sort of weather?

All this while he had not uttered a word, causing me to assume he was a deaf mute!

Fuming with rage I climbed down and set off down the lane he had indicated; I was certainly not going to pay the fellow for leaving me stranded in a raging blizzard!

On entering the lane I caught sight of a sign which I could just about make out from the weak light of the cab, it said 'Dark Lane'.

What an odd title; surely the locals could have devised a more suitable name for it?

However as I progressed further in I began to realise how apt it was; clay banks rose up on either side, towering above my head with gnarled trees, whose bare branches interlocked over it forming a tunnel!

There was little snow here and what there was seemed to have a life of its own suddenly spiralling up and moving aimlessly about.

The further down the lane I went the darker it became until it was impossible to see a hand in front of me!

Soon I heard the sound of running water and putting out my hand I felt the stone wall of a small bridge.

I crossed carefully; the water beneath the bridge splashed and gurgled as it flowed through; I shuddered involuntarily at the thought of falling in and being carried away to a watery grave!

Then the lane began to climb away again; but the banks either side were still higher than a man.

As I struggled up the hill it began to snow heavily again and I began to resemble a snowman as it clung to me.
Also the flakes settled on my eye lashes began to freeze making it even more difficult to see where I was going! Surely my Aunt's cottage can't be far now? I looked desperately about me for a light or some sign of habitation.

It was not until I reached the top of the hill that I saw a light away to the right of me; thank God civilization at last!
I made out a track going down towards where I had seen the light and followed it.
A sudden gust of wind struck me carrying the sound of men singing; what madness was this?
I became convinced that I was hallucinating due to fatigue as I was now nearly exhausted.

CHAPTER FOUR

    Coming round a bend in the track I saw amongst the trees a large building with light coming from its great windows; a surge of relief filled my being and I stumbled towards it.
The great bronze knocker was shaped like the head of a bearded man and I pounded it against the studded oak door with all my remaining strength.
After what seemed like an age the door was opened by a distinguished looking man with white hair wearing a long white robe.
He beckoned me to enter and I gratefully went into a large entrance hall where he bade me to sit down.
Then he sent for two of his brethren who helped me out of my wet coat and hat and I was taken into the Prior's rooms.
This was apparently a Cistercian Order where only the Prior was allowed to speak; he sat me in front of a welcome fire and sent for food and a cup of some sort of hot wine flavoured with honey!
All this time the singing had continued and I asked him what it was for; "it is Evensong my son," he replied; "however we send up continuous pleas for all the sinners of this world.
"We are especially diligent at this time as tomorrow is the Birthday of our Lord, so we will keep a vigil all through this night!"

    He stood up and bade me follow him to a flight of stone stairs that led to a turret room.
"You should be comfortable here, I hope our worship will not disturb you; with that he bade me good night and left the room.

A fire had been lit and the shadows flickered on the tapestries hanging on the walls as I undressed and climbed thankfully into bed.

However, even though I was extremely fatigued I could not sleep; there was something about that constant chanting that made me uneasy.

I couldn't put my finger on it, but there seemed to be an underlying threat in that music as if it would pervade my very soul and steal it away!

As the fire burnt down the room seemed to suddenly gain a deathly chill and I pulled the clothes over my head to keep it out.

That damned chanting was still going on and it was sometime in the small hours that I eventually drifted off into a troubled slumber.

CHAPTER FIVE

I awoke with a start wondering what was wrong; at first I couldn't think what it was, then I realised the chanting had stopped!
When I tried to push back the bedclothes my hand went through whatever was covering me; it was snow; whilst my bed was the stone floor of the chamber!
Jumping up I brushed myself down and looked around me; another shock awaited me; it was as light as day; mainly due to, the fact that the turret had no roof; the place was a ruin!
I looked out of the window onto the main body of the priory; that too was a ruin; hardly a stone left standing. My mind became numb, it was incapable of reason; was I mad or had I really spent the night in a place haunted by phantoms?
On examining myself I realized that I was fully dressed in my own clothes, which were wet with melted snow!

Hurrying down the stairs nearly proved my undoing as there were several steps missing; how had I got up there without breaking my neck?
A thousand questions swarmed around my brain until I thought it would burst as I struggled through the drifts towards the road.
On gaining Dark Lane once more I perceived two cottages about a hundred yards away' surely one of these must belong to my aunt?
Approaching me was a policeman on a bicycle; on seeing me he dismounted; "are you Mr. Goodwin sir," he asked?
"Yes I am," I replied.
"Thank God;" he said, "your aunt rang the station last night to report you missing, and in view of the weather we turned out to find you!"

"I wish you had found me last night;" I replied and proceeded to relate what had happened.

The constable's face was a study as my tale unfolded and he took off his helmet and scratched his head.

"Well sir that is a strange story and no mistake; I don't know what my sergeant will make of it, perhaps you would like to call in to Aylsham after Christmas so we can take a statement!"

With that he wished me the compliments of the Season; mounted his bike and wobbled off down the snowy road.

The bells of Aylsham church began to ring out over the water meadows reminding us it was Christmas Day as I trudged towards the two cottages.

CHAPTER SIX

My aunt was overjoyed to see me and threw her arms about my neck; "thank God you are safe my boy; where on earth did you get to?"
I once more described my ordeal and she listened attentively until I had finished; "but the Priory has become a ruin since the Reformation," she cried!
She then told me of how the Cistercian monks had been cruelly driven out by order of the King on Christmas Day 1538.
"The poor souls had to beg for a living and many actually starved;" she continued, "after all the devotion to the poor and needy they had given until that time!"
"I think you must have been the victim of a time warp; it seems strange that it was the night before their eviction.
Noticing the state of my clothes she sent me up for a hot bath, providing me with a dressing gown to cover my pyjamas whilst she dried my clothes by the fire.

After a hearty breakfast I began to feel more like my old self and attempted to make a fuss of Mr.Moggs; who responded by spitting at me and haughtily stalking out of the room!
We spent three happy days together; but all good things come to an end and I rang for a taxi to take me to Aylsham.
As we waited for its arrival I happened to mention the strange cab driver that had driven me through the snow that night.
My aunt looked puzzled; "the person you are describing sounds like old Joshua Medler; he used to pick up fares from the station in all kinds of weather."
"Why are you speaking about him in the past tense," I asked?

"Because he has been dead these past twenty years!" she replied.

THE END

CLOSE TO YOU

CHAPTER ONE

I dreamt of you again last night; a sort of muddled dream it was with wrong times and places interweaving the dream making it hard to grasp the real happenings from the fantasy!
We were down by the river and you were wriggling your bare toes in the water; your laughter sounding like tinkling silver bells; then that odious fellow Carl turned up and began to spoil everything.
He and I began to argue and I lost my temper and then the dream changed and we were back in the cottage; you were ill in bed and the place was cold as ice.
I had lost my job and couldn't afford to pay for coal; I took an axe into the Estate and started cutting up branches for firewood.
The Gamekeeper caught me and tried to take the axe off me; then in the dream we were going to Cromer on the wagon; we were happy and looking forward to a day by the sea; you snuggled up to me and the others pretended not to notice!
Suddenly it became dark and I could not find you! I looked everywhere and called your name, but try as I might it was to no avail.
Then I awoke and lay in the darkness aware of the tears trickling down my face; oh! where are you my love; come back to me, come back to me!

Another dreary day without you my love; the same predictable, unimaginative waiting for night and my dreams to come and rescue me.

That is when I feel close to you my sweet; I see you and sometimes hold you in my arms, only to be torn from you when I awake!
It seems an eternity since we were together and happy in each others company; I felt that I was the luckiest man alive to have you for my love.
Then that black day arrived when Carl came into our lives and from that time I began to lose you!
I hated the man from the first; with his superior manner and flashy clothes; worst of all was his unwelcome attentions towards you.
I cannot blame you for being flattered by his attention and impressed by his false generosity; he swept you off your feet I guess!
I had to stand by while he stole your affection for me away; how could I compete with all he could offer!
The many lonely nights I waited for your return; knowing that you were with him and forgetting about me.
It became unbearable and I began to have dark thoughts about getting rid of him so you would come back to me and we would be happy again!

CHAPTER TWO

   I managed to get a job at the local slaughter house; it was cruel, dirty work and I hated it; but it paid well and I tried to buy nice things for you so you would come back to me; but to no avail.
You would wrinkle your pretty little nose when I came near you and made excuses when I asked you to come out with me.
Carl took great delight in humiliating me and boasting about what he had bought for you and where he had taken you!
 I began to drink heavily and spent more and more time in the tavern associating with idle fellows who pretended to be my friends.
They started to ridicule me behind my back and words like cuckold and simpleton were often mentioned till I could stand it no longer; one night I fought one of them and got a knife slash on my cheek for my troubles!
After that I became a recluse and shunned my fellow men; I lost my cottage as I had been sacked from my job and couldn't pay the rent.
I slept rough in barns and haystacks and got work where I could; but I never forgot you or stopped loving you.

   My wanderings took me all over the country and it was many years before I found myself back in Norfolk. I came back to the village; but I had changed in appearance so much that no one recognised this old bundle of rags with a great beard (which I had grown to cover the scar on my cheek) and a wrinkled weather beaten face.
I got a job with the local Thatcher; renewing the thatch on the great barn on the Estate; he was a skilful man,

but a hard task master and kept me working from morning till night.

However he allowed me to sleep in his reed store, which was warm and cosy and his missus sent me a pasty for my snap, so it wasn't so bad!

On the Sunday I had the afternoon off and made some enquiries as to where Carl lived; it turned out that he rented a cottage next to the blacksmith's forge.

I walked up the street till I came to it and there were two small children playing in the front garden.

They were engrossed in their play and I stopped to watch them; innocent little things they were blissfully unaware of what a cruel world they had been brought into!

Just then a fierce dog rushed out of the gate at me followed by its master Carl. He shouted; "be off with you we don't want your sort in the village!"

I closed my fist and brought it down hard on the dog's head; it yelped and fell half stunned onto the ground; I had got used to dealing with aggressive dogs on my travels.

Carl began to bluster; "I'll have the law on you for attacking my dog; if he's injured you will pay for it!"

"You set the dog on me on the Kings Highway, that is an offence;" I replied.

He stopped and looked hard at me; "do I know you?" he said.

I laughed bitterly and replied; "maybe in another life;" and turned and continued on my way, leaving him standing in the road looking thoughtful.

We finished thatching the barn just before Michaelmass, so I said goodbye to the Thatcher and his missus and started to leave the village as there was nothing to hold me now!

CHAPTER THREE

As I reached the forge who should be standing there in the road but Carl with a whip in his hand!
"I know now who you are!" he shouted; "comin sniffin' round my house; I know what you're after!"
"Do you now;" I replied, all that was years ago and I have to accept the situation."
I made to walk round him and felt the lash of his whip cut into my shoulder.
"You don't fool me with your mealy mouthed excuses; I'm goin to give you a lesson you'll never forget!"
He made to whip me again and I caught the tip in my hand and pulled him towards me.
By now all the suppressed anger and bitterness had welled up inside me and I totally lost my temper!
This man had taken everything that I loved away from me and it was as if I had been given the strength of ten men!

Carl was a big man, but I caught him by the throat and lifted him off the ground squeezing the life out of him; the blood from my hand was running down his neck as he struggled in vain to free himself, soon he was still and I let him fall to the ground.
I felt drained of all emotion as I walked on up the street; the magnitude of what I had done did not strike me at first; my one desire was to put as much distance between me and that accursed place as I could!
The police caught up with me and I was taken to Norwich prison to await the Assizes.
I knew the gallows awaited me and looked forward to it as a happy release from my tormented mind
The trial came and went in a blur of accusations and recriminations by various relatives of the deceased; but

the one sweet face I longed to see was not amongst them!
You have abandoned me and God has turned his face from me because of my awful sin; I have deprived you of a husband and your children of a father in a fit of jealous rage!

   The day of my execution dawned and I was taken into a shed adjoining the prison where the deed was to be done.
There was a small crowd of witnesses as well as the Governor and the priest and a murmur arose as I was brought up the steps to the gallows!
A senior warder checked my bonds and placed me over the trap door; whilst the clergyman read suitable passages from the Bible.
Then the hangman put the hood over my head and I felt the knot of the rope under my left ear.
I was still thinking of you as I fell through the trapdoor into oblivion!

CHAPTER FOUR

   So here I am trapped between this world and the next, seemingly doomed to wander without forgiveness, a lost soul unable to share human company; but my feelings for you are still as strong as ever!
I often oversee you when you are with your children; watching them growing up and seeing how you love them.
I cannot help thinking that it would have been perfect if they had been ours and I could have shared in the happiness that children bring.
However I lost that chance so many years ago when we drifted apart, my only consolation is that I have been given the gift of being able to visit you on occasion.
Your little girl can see me and she talks to me sometimes; but I don't like to be too intrusive in case she becomes frightened!
   As the years go by I find it more difficult to visit you and I wonder if there is a change in my state coming so that it will be denied me?
I could not bear that as my dearest wish is that one day in spirit finally, I shall always be close to you!

THE END

BLACK FEN

CHAPTER ONE

The snow came about seven that evening: it had been threatening all day with leaden skies and a gusting wind.
I looked at Peter and said: "I reckon we shall have to think about calling it a day; he nodded as he opened the car door and pulled his coat around him.
He was an agent for the Insurance Company I worked for and we had been canvassing for business in the Wisbech area without much success!
"The trouble is Jim;"he said; "the folks round here only invest in land when they have any spare money; that way they can increase their wealth by growing more crops!"
We had stopped down one of the unmade roads called droves; of which there are many in this region.
An isolated bungalow stood before us and I noticed there were no lights showing; "I reckon there's nobody in;" I said.
Just then the door opened and a man called out; "is that you Peter?"
"Come in, we're just lighting the lamps as the electricity has just gone;" he said.
Apparently this is not uncommon as the overhead power lines are exposed to the constant battering by the winds in this flat region.
We had a chat and eventually I asked him if we could help him with information regarding pensions or investment.
He smiled and said; "no thanks all the same; we've just bought a couple of acres of arable land down near Emneth!"

I looked at Peter and gave a rueful smile; I stood up, shook his hand, made our excuses and went out to the car.

The snow was beginning to lay and I became concerned about getting home; my house was on the other side of Norwich, about fifty miles away!
"If you don't mind Peter I'll run you home; I expect they could do with you there if the power is off!"
It was quite a way back to the old cottage where he lived; it stood on a narrow road with deep dykes on either side of the road full of rippling cold dark water. I shuddered involuntarily; thinking of the tales I had heard of unsuspecting motorists ending up in one of these things and drowning!
He jumped out and waved as I drove away; by now the snow was being driven horizontally by the roaring wind across the desolate fens and I began to regret not leaving sooner.
As I drove along the isolated empty roads with the wooden electricity poles leaning at odd angles a feeling of dark depression stole over me; there seemed to be a silent hostility about this region which was almost palpable!
It was now getting dark and my headlights were of little help; as the falling snow obliterated the beams; I was forced to a crawl; being very aware of the cold dark dykes either side of me!
I began to panic; what if I became stranded? In this weather it was doubtful if there would be many travellers on this desolate road, and finding a dwelling in this rural wasteland was unlikely!
However; just at that moment a light shone faintly through the snow ahead and as I approached I glimpsed a beech hedge and a gate with a board above it proclaiming Bed and Breakfast.

Salvation; I decided that I would stay the night and travel home the next day.

   I drove in and pulled up outside an old farmhouse; it had seen better days and looked as if some of the outbuildings had fallen down!
Never mind, any port in a storm I thought; I walked up to the Gothic style studded door and pulled the handle of the door bell.

CHAPTER TWO

There was a muffled jangling noise from deep within the house and eventually the door was partially opened and a burly man peered out.
"What do you want?" he asked suspiciously.
"Shelter for the night if you please;" I said pulling my coat collar up as the snow fell down the back of my neck!
He grunted and opened the door; I followed the light of his oil lamp down a gloomy corridor noting various stuffed birds under glass covers and several oil paintings hanging on the wainscoting.
He led me into a large room, which again seemed to be furnished in the Edwardian style with glass cabinets containing china plate and figurines.
He bade me sit down on an old chesterfield and disappeared into the bowels of the house; I could hear him moving around and the sound of crockery being rattled!
He came back bearing a welcome cup of tea which I gratefully drank.
"I'm afraid that since my mother died I don't have many guests;" he said almost apologetically!
"That's OK," I said; "I'm just glad of somewhere to lay my head for the night in this appalling weather!"
"Have you far to go?" he enquired.
"Norwich;" I replied; "but I don't think I'd have made it in this weather!"
He appeared to consider my remarks, but made no comment.
"If you would like to follow me I will show you your room;" he picked up the lamp and went to the door; I hurried after him as we made for the stairs.
The lamp threw grotesque shadows on the walls as we walked up the staircase and I noticed the place smelt

musty as if it were riddled with damp; indeed some of the wallpaper was beginning to peel.
We arrived outside a panelled door which he threw open and directed me inside; it had a high moulded ceiling and a large double bed.
"This is the guest bedroom;" he said as if he had carefully rehearsed it; "the bathroom is down the corridor to your left.
Having delivered this information he turned suddenly and left the room; there was a guttering candle on the bedside cabinet which provided the sole source of light.
I drew back the heavy brocade curtains and looked out of the window; it had stopped snowing and the moon was shining, making it as light as day!
The snow lay deep and I noticed that the house almost backed onto a large expanse of water surrounded by trees, whose gnarled branches seemed to reach out over the water as if in supplication!
There were footprints in the snow and I was intrigued to note that they seemed to come from the direction of the fen!
The hair on the back of my neck rose; what did this mean; the place was creepy enough in its own right and as for mine host; to say the least he was odd!
I got undressed and climbed into bed; the sheets felt damp and try as I might I could not get to sleep.
I lay there with the moon shining across the bedroom floor with a thousand unanswered questions whirling around in my head!
What is the secret of this place; who's are the footprints in the snow; why do they come from the fen?
   I thought I could here someone talking downstairs; the cadence of the voice kept rising and falling like a form of chanting!

Perhaps he has religious mania I thought; a picture of him kneeling on the floor with hands clasped and eyes raised heavenwards flashed before me.
Then the chanting stopped and I heard footsteps coming up the stairs; then slowly the handle of the bedroom door began to turn!

CHAPTER THREE

I slipped quickly out of bed slipping the bolster under the sheets to look as if I were still there and hid behind the door.
The door opened slowly and the man entered the room; something in his hand flashed in the moonlight, it was a knife!
He crept up to the bed and raising the knife high above his head brought it down and plunged it into the covers where I had left the bolster.
He stabbed it again and again in a frenzied attack; finally pulling back the sheets to examine his handywork!
On seeing the bolster he let out a howl of anguish and turned; the moonlight lit up his contorted face; his eyes bulged and saliva dripped from his mouth; the man was totally deranged!
Seeing me standing behind him he raised his knife and made a rush at me; in the process he tripped over the sheets on the floor and fell heavily!
I went to take the knife from him only to discover it buried deeply in his chest; he must have fallen on it and he was dead!
I went in search of a phone; but there was no sign of one in the house; downstairs I noticed wet footprints leading to the back door which was open.
I looked out just in time to see something moving towards the fen; it disappeared amongst the trees at the fringe of the water and I swear I heard a splash!
I went back into the house and found a bottle of whisky on the sideboard and poured myself a large one to calm my nerves; what a predicament: the police would naturally be suspicious as I was the only other person in the house.

Then again if I just left the house forensics would find finger prints and traces of my DNA and be convinced that I had killed him!
I don't know what made me pick up a diary from the bureau; I idly flipped the pages as I sipped my drink. As I read it I could not believe my eyes; this man believed there was an entity living in the fen!
Not only that; he claimed to be an acolyte of this creature and freely admitted that he had to kill people to appease the thing's blood lust!
The man was obviously delusional and a dangerous psychopath to boot; I had had a lucky escape!
I must have finished the whole bottle as I awoke with a start to see it was day and a watery sun was struggling to pierce the clouds.

   I dressed and went out to the car intending to go to Wisbech and report the matter to the local police.
The roads were still tricky and it took me a long while to reach the town; the first thing I did was to phone my wife; she sounded relieved to hear from me; I told her that I had put up for the night due to the weather; but did not elaborate; she was worried enough without hearing the gory details of last night's episode!
Then I drove to the police station and related my story to the desk sergeant; he obviously thought that it was a matter for the inspector and I was ushered into his office.
"Now then sir;" he said ponderously; "pr'aps you would like to start at the beginning and tell me what this is all about!"
I began all over again whilst he made notes at what he thought were salient points of my story.
When I had finished he put his fingertips together and looking hard at me said accusingly; "how much had you been drinking last night sir?"

I exploded; "look man there is a body lying on the bedroom floor; I tell you the man attempted to kill me whilst I slept; this has nothing to do with drink!"

CHAPTER FOUR

"That is as maybe;" he said significantly; "but we have enough to do as it is without gallivanting round the countryside on wild goose chases sir!"
I didn't like the emphasis he put on sir; it sounded like an insult; I stood up; "well if that is your attitude inspector I shall take it to a higher authority!"
That gave him pause for thought; "Let's not be hasty sir; we have a lot of time wasters and hoaxers to deal with;" catching the expression on my face he hurriedly added; "present company excepted of course sir; I will personally take charge of this at once."
He put on his hat and coat and beckoning me to follow swept into the main office and called two constables to accompany us.
We drove off in a police car to the B&B, which apparently was called Black Fen Farm!

As we swept up the drive it looked more derelict than ever in daylight with it's windows looking like empty eye sockets, peering blankly at the world.
The front door was locked so I took them round to the back of the house; the snow was now beginning to melt and the footprints were becoming indistinct.
However there was a swathe of flattened snow going all the way down to the waters edge with a red stained trail in it!
My heart gave a lurch and I suppressed the thought that had entered my head; we went up to the bedroom and my worst fears had been realised; the body had gone!
The inspector stood with arms akimbo and an expression that made me think of official retribution for time wasters!
"Look Inspector there is a large blood stain on the carpet;" said one of the constables, and knelt down to feel whether it was still wet, which it was.

"That's where he fell;" I blurted out with relief;
however that was short lived!
"Where have you disposed of the body?" the inspector
snapped.
"I haven't done anything with it;" I protested; "so help
me it was here when I left this morning!"
"We only have your word for that;" he retorted;
"Constable cuff him and read him his rights.
"Just a minute;" I protested; "there's no evidence
against me and I deny killing him, he fell on his knife!"
"And you have no evidence to prove that; where is the
knife and where are your witnesses?"

  It was hopeless; the inspector had made up his mind
that I had killed the man; there was no knife and no
body and as I was the only suspect; ergo sum, as far as
he was concerned I was in the hot seat!
The journey back to Wisbech was conducted in silence;
whilst my mind worked overtime trying to think of
some way of proving my innocence.
I was allowed one phone call and I spoke to my wife
who went into hysterics; after calming her down
somewhat I asked her to contact our solicitor and ask
him to organise a brief for me.
She wanted to come over to be with me; but I
persuaded her that it would be counter productive and
we would have to get someone to look after the kids!
The interrogation seemed to go on and on, until I
became bewildered and exhausted, they got me to sign
a statement; by which time I would have signed
anything just to make it stop!
My brief arrived in the afternoon and went over the
case with me; after a while I began to get the
impression that he didn't believe me either!

Then I remembered the diary! Of course that would prove the man was a candidate for the 'funny farm' and I was the innocent party.

   The police retrieved the diary and subsequently dragged the fen; finding the remains of several bodies, including that of Mr.Roberts that I was supposed to have killed!
The knife was still in his chest; the strange thing was that all the bodies had teeth marks all over them as if they had been gnawed by a large animal!
There were also human bones scattered all over the bottom of the fen, which on examination proved to be several hundred years old; all exhibiting teeth marks.
The Post Mortem was closed to the public, much to the annoyance of the Press!
I was released without further charge and returned to my work with an unblemished record.
Black Fen Farm was later pulled down after an old tramp; who had been 'dossing' there for several days disappeared without trace other that a well worn pair of brown boots which had seen better days!
As for me; I have a gentleman's agreement with my boss that I do not work in the fens any more!

THE END

LAST TRAIN TO HEYDON

CHAPTER ONE

Joseph Mears felt pleased with himself as he settled into his seat on the last train to Heydon.
He had only just managed to catch his connection as the London train had been late.
What a wonderful day he had had, visiting the Great Exhibition at the Crystal Palace; mingling with people of quality as well as the 'great unwashed.'
He marvelled at the wonderful things he had seen in the Great Hall; inventions from all over the world.
He was a watchmaker by trade and although he had been born and raised in the village of Heydon his shop was in the adjacent Market Town of Reepham.
He listened whilst the rhythm of the tracks became more insistent as the engine gathered speed on leaving Norwich station.
He looked at his gold hunter and perceived that it was a quarter to twelve, he sighed
it seemed as if he would have to walk from the station to his cottage in the village!
The occasional cloud of steam caressed the window as the train sped along and the night reflected his image on the carriage window.

The experience of the day in London dominated his thoughts; what an experience, so different to the mundane existence he was forced to lead in this rural backwater!
Joseph imagined himself running a successful business in Bond Street with a fine carriage to take him back to his large house in Knightsbridge where a pretty young wife would be waiting to attend to his every whim.

The fact that he was still a bachelor at fifty, rather stout and bald into the bargain seemed to indicate that his expectations rather exceeded his chances of achieving them!
However at this moment of time he was supremely happy and looked forward to regaling his acquaintances at the Earl Arms with tales of London life and the Great Exhibition.
Lights were appearing on either side of the carriage as the train drew into Cawston station.

   A few people alighted and began walking down the platform in and out of the pools of
light created by the gas lamps as they went.
The discordant noise of milk churns being unloaded onto the platform from the train roused Joseph from his reverie.
Finally the guard blew his whistle and the train jerked forward panting like an eager dog on a leash!
He gathered his few possessions together as the next stop was Bluestone from whence he would be walking home.
He pulled the leather strap to lower the window and looked out as the train pulled into the small station.
The platform was empty with the porters barrows stacked against the railings, he checked his watch again and noted it had just gone a quarter to one.
Alighting, he shut the carriage door and began to walk towards the exit; the wind had begun to rise and scudding clouds were racing across the face of a bright full moon.
There was no carrier's cart outside which was hardly surprising at this time of night.
He resigned himself to walking home and followed the track towards the Holt road.

CHAPTER TWO

It was as light as day and the moonlight flooded the woods on either side showing every bush and tree!
On reaching the road he crossed and entered the gateway of the wood cutters cottage and began to follow the path that would take him through Bluestone woods.
The further he went the more nervous he became; pouring into his mind came stories of murder, night owlers and ghosts!
There were many old wives tales relating to the woods most of which were either pure imagination or told to disobedient children to dissuade them from straying too far in and getting lost!
However when a person is walking through a forest in the middle of the night it is difficult to distinguish between imagination and common sense!
Joseph nearly jumped out of his skin as a nearby owl hooted accusingly at him and again when a fox ran across the path into the undergrowth.
He peered anxiously around him as he quickened his step wishing that he had caught an earlier train.
Oh it had been easy to be brave and foolhardy during daylight hours, but now confronted with his surroundings and the unfamiliar noises around him it was a different matter indeed!
A twig snapped behind him causing him to spin round to see what was about to spring on his back.
He caught a fleeting glimpse of a pair of eyes glinting in the bush then they were gone.
Joseph began to tremble and redoubled his pace, as he rounded a bend in the path he tripped and fell over a rotten branch lying across it.
The fall knocked the wind out of him and he lay for some minutes trying to regain his breath.

That was when he heard the strange sounds coming from his left; it was like a dog ravenously attacking a carcass!

He cautiously raised his head and looked across to where the sound was coming from.

A beam of moonlight lit up a clearing where he perceived a figure hunched over something lying on the ground.

The slobbering, tearing sounds were interspersed with grunts of what sounded like satisfaction!

Suddenly the figure stopped and turned towards him, the blood covered face belonged to a man!

Joseph was paralysed with fear, his legs would not respond to the overwhelming desire to escape.

They gazed at one another for what seemed an age until Joseph's legs became mobile again; he leapt to his feet emitting a loud scream and ran as fast as his short legs would carry him, leaving the creature still crouching over its half eaten prey snarling defiantly!

As he ran the picture of the man's bloody appearance and animal like behaviour was burnt into his mind and he listened as he ran for any sounds of pursuit!

Bursting through the undergrowth he came out on the foreshore of the lake; the moon's reflection shimmered off the water and dead branches of trees stuck out of the water like the despairing arms of drowning men!

There was a small boathouse to his left and he ran desperately towards it, there was a small rowing boat inside.

He jumped in and picking up the oar he attempted to push off, the boat would not move; in his haste he had forgotten to cast off the mooring rope!

Almost sobbing with terror he undid the knot with trembling fingers and tried once more to push the boat out into the lake.

This time he succeeded and sitting down he began to row towards the opposite side.
His spirits began to rise as he rowed; he had made his escape from whatever it was!

   Suddenly there was a terrible cry from the side of the lake he had just left; he nearly dropped the oars in the water; slowly he turned round, his mind full of dread and sure enough, looking terrible in the moonlight, stood the creature with arms outstretched and a look of madness on it's awful face.

CHAPTER THREE

Joseph was transfixed and could not take his eyes off it as the little boat drifted aimlessly in the centre of the lake.
After a long stare the creature turned and loped off into the wood, Joseph regained some of his erstwhile composure and picking up the oars he made for the far shore.
Reaching it he jumped out of the boat leaving it to drift away while he walked quickly towards the nearby farmhouse where he intended to seek refuge!
Soon he spied the heart warming lights of the dwelling just across the field and quickened his pace as he left the wood and began to cross the path to safety.
Arriving at the house he began hammering on the door, casting fearful glances behind him as he did so.
What was taking the occupants so long to answer, they must have heard his desperate knocking; it was loud enough to awaken the dead!
The door suddenly gave under his hand and swung open silently revealing a lighted hallway, he gratefully entered and shut the door behind him,
Slipping the bolts across to lock the door he walked down the passage calling as he went.
He walked into the kitchen and beheld a sight that nearly made him faint; slumped in a chair beside the table was the farmer, his head was thrown back revealing that his throat had been torn out!

Joseph felt sick at the terrible sight, he reached out to the table to steady himself, as he did so there came a thunderous pounding on the door.
His heart nearly leapt out of his chest; the beast had found him; he was doomed!

From somewhere he found the courage to shout, 'go away and leave me alone, you cannot get in I have bolted the door!'
A muffled voice from outside shouted, 'it's all right sir we are the police, please unlock the door.
He rushed to the door and opened it; sure enough there was a sergeant and two constables waiting.
Joseph babbled with relief, plying them with questions as they entered the house.
The sergeant took him into the living room and sat him down.
'Your tribulations are over sir,' he said, 'we apprehended the man shortly after you abandoned the boat.'
As a matter of fact it was hearing your cry that led us to him; we have been on his trail since he escaped from Norwich lunatic asylum on Wednesday!'
'What sort of madman is he to go around the countryside behaving like a wild animal,'
asked Joseph?'
The sergeant smiled, 'who knows sir, he is normally docile, but when there is a full moon he reverts to the creature that you saw!'
'How did he get out,' asked Joseph, surely he should be kept in secure surroundings?'
'Normally he is,' said the sergeant, 'but on this particular day he was being transferred to a different cell and he overpowered his guard and escaped!'
'During these phases he develops almost superhuman strength and it takes several men to hold him down!.
 Joseph shuddered.he had obviously had a narrow escape, which is more than could be said for the farmer!
'Will you be alright going home sir?'
Joseph nodded absently, still thinking of what might have happened to him, he rose and made for the door.

'Would you call in to Reepham police station tomorrow sir," called the sergeant;. 'we will need a statement from you!'

'Yes,' replied Joseph, still in a daze as he set out for his home, the moon was still shining, lighting his way along the road.

He was still afraid and kept shooting glances at the hedges each side of the road; he did not think that he would ever get over the ordeal, that face still haunted his mind!

Unlocking his front door he stumbled into his kitchen and opened a cupboard producing a bottle of brandy he poured himself a liberal glass full and tossed it down his throat; tea was definitely not the beverage for a night like this!

He undressed and climbed gratefully in to bed, but sleep eluded him as each time he closed his eyes that face appeared!

He dozed fitfully until dawn then got up and readied himself for the day ahead.

CHAPTER FOUR

At the police station he was ushered into the sergeant's office where he wrote out his statement. The sergeant read it and put it into a wooden tray, he seemed in an expansive mood and leaning over the desk he began to tell Joseph more about the man they had captured.
'The chief warder at the Institution told me that he came from a well to do family; as is traditional he was sent on the Grand Tour of Europe!"
"After travelling through France to Italy he came home via Hungary and stayed with a Count in Transylvania."
"The Count had organised a shoot on his forested estate, somehow our man got separated from the rest of the shooting party and it was late evening before they found him wandering in the forest".
"He claimed to have been attacked by a wolf and it had bitten him several times before he managed to fight it off."
"He was taken back to the castle and had his wounds attended to, seeming to make a speedy recovery."
"However on returning to his family seat he became more and more morose and withdrawn."

"One night during the phase of the full moon his father heard strange noises coming from his son's bedroom."
"On investigation he found the place in disarray and the window wide open; of his son there was no sign!"
"In fear of his safety his father organised a search party of estate workers who scoured the land around looking for him without success".
"The next morning his father went to his son's room and discovered him huddled in a corner, his clothes

were torn and soiled, his eyes were wild and his face was covered in blood!".

"He was bathed and washed and put to bed till the doctor arrived; the doctor examined him and then called the father out into the corridor".

'Where did your son get those bite marks, he enquired, they look as if he was savaged by a dog!'

'The father explained what had happened during his son's travels'.

'Hmm; 'mused the doctor, 'it's a good job I'm not a believer in old superstitions otherwise I might be inclined to think it was a case of lycanthropy!'

'What may that be,' asked the father being puzzled by the term.

The doctor smiled; 'have you never heard of werewolves sir?'

The father was outraged; 'what are you inferring doctor that my son turns into a wolf; that is preposterous and unprofessional!'

The doctor raised his hands; 'please sir I do not think anything of the kind, what I do believe is that he needs the advice of a specialist who deals with illness of the mind!'

"So the unfortunate man was eventually committed after several years of treatment failed to resolve the matter."

The sergeant leaned back and smiled at Joseph; 'so there you have the reason why he has to be detained indefinitely in an institution for the insane.'

'What if he escapes again,' said Joseph?

'Oh, he has escaped several times and no doubt when the moon is full again he will make another attempt to free himself, but we will ensure that he does not succeed; now if you will excuse me sir I have other duties to attend to, good day to you!'

Joseph left the police station feeling very insecure after hearing the revelation that the man had escaped on more than one occasion.
Suppose he returned to Bluestone wood and killed again; he realised that he had not asked what the man was dining on when he first encountered him!
He unlocked the door of his shop in the market place and tried his best to concentrate on his work; surely that would help him to return to normality?
So dear reader if you must catch the last train to Heydon either take the long way round or carry a gun with silver bullets; failing that make sure the moon is not full!

THE END